KINGDOM FORGOTTEN

☽☽☽

BOOK 2 | THE DESTINY COLLECTION

Leslie Redden

Dream
Reach
Fly

LESLIE REDDEN

ISBN: 1497438985
ISBN 13: 978-1497438989
Library of Congress Control Number: 2014906541
CreateSpace Independent Publishing Platform
North Charleston, South Carolina

Cover Design: Cory & Abby Egan & Tyler & Leslie Redden

**Dedicated
To My Loving Husband
Thank you for your continued patience
through yet another book creation.**

I Love You!

1

CORBETT

Corbett scanned the empty cabin that he had called home for so many years. The emptiness seemed to settle quietly as he closed the front door for the final time. Two copper-colored horses, Titian and Umber; the wagon; a few household items; and two wooden rocking chairs that his father carved were all that he had. Corbett stopped at the gate and waited a few minutes for the new owners to arrive. As they rode their horses down the road, he gazed at the key in his hand. For a moment, he questioned his decision to sell the house he grew up in, but he dismissed it just as quickly, knowing his parents would have wanted him to live a life he would be happy with. As his cousin Sam and his cousin's wife, Em, approached, Corbett walked over to them with thoughtful steps.

He squeezed the plain silver key tightly in his strong hand, somehow feeling closer to his parents as he did. "Here is the key to your new home. I hope you enjoy it as much as my family and I did." He handed the key to Sam and blinked back a few tears from his crystal-blue eyes.

"Oh, we are so excited! I can't wait to put all our things in the house. The land will be such a blessing for establishing our future with a farm. Thank you again for the incredible piece of land and the home," the plump young wife, Em, said with such excitement she became short of breath.

"You are welcome. Enjoy it, and I hope it is as much of a blessing to you as it has been to me and my parents." Corbett shook hands with Em and gave Sam a quick hug.

"The family will miss you. Thank you again."

Corbett looked at his childhood home one last time. He would miss the life he had here but knew his memories would be with him for the rest of his life. He waved good-bye to the giddy couple, then turned his horses toward the direction of his new life, east.

He thought of his parents as he plodded along the road. They would have both been proud of their only child for not only finding a carpentry job but also a new place to live. After his father passed away a month ago, Corbett contacted some of his father's acquaintances in Gilleran, inquiring about any work. He had not expected a quick response, but to his surprise, a week later a note came.

Dear Corbett,

Your father once told me you are as talented (if not more so) as he in woodworking. If you will accept the offer, you are hired in my lumber mill upon delivery of this letter. Please join me in Gilleran at my residence, and I will have a place for you to live. Your father was more than an acquaintance to me— he was a dear friend. It would honor me in knowing that I am providing a good life for my old friend's son.

Sincerely, William

P.S. I already have a project for you.

Corbett had read the letter with awe. The last line of the letter sparked his curiosity. What could William mean by *a project*? At his father's funeral, Corbett had spoken with his aunt Milda about what to do with the home if he ever moved. She had wished him to stay as long as he wanted and offered to move in with him since he was only sixteen; he would be turning seventeen in a few months. It was decided by the family that his cousin Sam and his wife, Em, would buy his home for a minimal fee when the time came for him to move. He felt relieved that the home would stay in the family, and a little extra money would help him whenever he did move. He had not known starting a new life would happen so quickly.

The day began to wane, giving way to a crisp breeze. Corbett pulled his wagon over near a group of old cottonwoods. He unhitched the horses and tethered them loosely to some young saplings near a small brook. He started a small fire and made rabbit stew for dinner, accompanied by some sweet rolls Milda had made for him. Closing his eyes, he savored the warm, fresh stew in the cool evening air. His two horses munched quietly on the green grass, and the leaves lightly rustled in the evening breeze.

Corbett thought of his mother and father, and a few tears escaped his eyes, landing in his stew. His parents had both died of old age—his mother first, followed by his father just a month ago. He had been the only child to Em and Bill. They were known in the family for doting on all their nieces and nephews, having given up on ever having children because of their age. Corbett smiled to himself as he remembered his mother's voice speaking of his birth on his birthday every April. His parents adored him and raised him to be the responsible young man he had become. He hoped he would continue to make them proud with his new life. He shivered as the light of his fire had died to all but a smolder. His horses slept quietly near the wagon. He grabbed a few blankets and made a bed in the back of the wagon. He slipped into a sweet sleep, remembering the love his parents had given him, letting a few warm tears escape down his cheeks.

He opened his eyes to a sunny spring day. It was not warm but beautiful. While stretching, Titian and Umber greeted him with their big quiet eyes. He knew they wanted some morning oats. He ate a little bread with honey for breakfast, fed his horses, and began his journey to Gilleran. He calculated how far he had traveled, figuring he should reach Gilleran by nightfall unless he encountered a problem along the way, which he didn't foresee happening.

Gilleran rose in the faint distance with spots of glass reflecting in the dimming sun as he rode to the top of a small hill. The town looked large as he gazed at it from the hill. It sprawled and stopped abruptly at a massive forest. He had made great time, only having to stop a few times to stretch his legs. As he began the descent down the hill, his horses started to get skittish.

"Shh...boys, don't worry it is only a forest. Nothing in there to worry about."

They calmed a little at his voice, walked a few more steps, and then stopped, refusing to walk any farther. Corbett knew to pay attention to his horses, so he put the break on the wagon. The horses' nostrils flared as they stared intently into the darkening forest. He stood near their heads, staring into the forest, trying to see what they saw. He took a few steps forward and stopped. There, at the edge of the forest, a silver glimmer caught his eye. He walked backward to his horses and held their lead. The last thing he wanted was for all his belongings to be strewn across the hill. The silver glimmer disappeared, and a figure suddenly appeared in the center of the road. The figure was tall with a black hooded cape covering its features. Something silver caught Corbett's attention again. It appeared to be the blade of a sword. Corbett stood his ground, not knowing what would come next. A cackle of laughter surged unnaturally from the figure, which seemed to be a shadow of a man. Corbett held tightly to the lead as the horses spooked.

He slowly walked toward the figure as he moved his free hand to his bow nestled on his back.

The shadowy man spoke in an eerie song: "You... gifted one, will see. He comes."

A flash came from the direction of the dark figure before Corbett knew what to do. The horses bolted. Corbett gripped tightly to the lead, but it whipped through his hands as the wagon began to slide sideways. A loud crack reverberated from the wagon, causing everything around Corbett to become muffled. In the confusion, he tripped and fell on his back. It took him a second to catch his breath.

He stood slowly and gazed at his wagon sitting at an awkward angle on top of the hill. *At least it didn't fall on its side,* he thought. Far down the road, in the direction he had just come from, he could see his horses. He felt frustrated that he would have to spend another night outside but thankful his wagon had not lost all of its contents. He wondered about the sound that had muffled his hearing. If it hadn't been the wagon falling over, what had it been? He picked up his clothes and household items that had flown out of the wagon during the confusion. Corbett looked at the forest again and saw nothing, no figure. He wanted to walk down the hill and investigate right then but knew that would be unwise. Who knew what would await him in the quickly fading daylight of the forest.

What had the voice meant? "Gifted one will see. He comes," he pondered as he walked with heavy, tired steps toward his horses.

"Shh...boys, you're not in trouble. You didn't have to run so far though." He spoke quietly to his horses as he got them settled.

The sun had disappeared behind some clouds, and night was settling in early around them. He lit a lantern and began inspecting the wagon. He stopped as he circled the last side. A long silver blade stuck out of the wagon. He reached to pull it out, and a flash of a dark castle sprung into his mind as he touched the cold silver hilt. It sent shivers through him. He let go and blinked at the sword. "Hmm...I think I have had a long day." He touched it again, and it had the same effect. His skin began to crawl. He looked for a cloth, something, anything, and found a blanket. He hesitantly touched the cold silver sword and nothing happened. He held it like it was a snake about to bite him and climbed into the wagon. He lay down to sleep, staring at the strange silver blade, focusing on the rubies that lined the hilt. He didn't sleep well, afraid of what would happen if he did fall into a deep sleep.

He felt exhausted by the time the first rays of sun appeared in the sky but relieved to know he would be in Gilleran by the end of the day. He worked quickly for being so tired. He had everything ready, but before he jumped up into his seat, he carefully grabbed the silver sword out of the back of the wagon. He did not want that thing, even if it did look impressive in the morning light as the sun gleamed off its silvery sharp sides with shining red rubies. It seemed a thing of dark beauty. He had passed a waterfall not far down the road the previous day. He climbed into his seat, careful not to touch any part of the sword, afraid those strange images from the previous night would appear again, and he drove in the opposite direction of Gilleran for a few miles. He could hear the fall's water gushing louder as he rode closer. He tethered his horses a little off the road, wrapped the hilt with an old cloth and walked with the mysterious sword. The green grass ended at a rocky precipice that looked over the large waterfall, and its cool water misted Corbett's face. He looked one last time at the strange sword and threw it over the embankment, watching the sun glint off the blade as it tumbled down. He stayed focused on the deep water below until he was certain the sword had sunk to its watery grave. Once satisfied, he turned and walked back to his wagon and jumped in. He started toward Gilleran and paused for a moment. He thought he heard something that did not quite fit with his surroundings. He didn't know what he had heard, but the sound disappeared and he began riding toward Gilleran.

The sword mysteriously floated toward the surface of the water, allowing a loud pop of bubbles to be heard as the pressure propelled the strange sword to the surface. The depths of the river did not want the sword either, and it began floating heavily down the river.

2

GILLERAN

Corbett passed through the dark forest without incident. Nothing to show for the previous night's trial, he let out a sigh of relief as he neared the gates of Gilleran, riding into the bright daylight. He pulled out his small map and located William's home. The town of Gilleran bustled with people, and the low gurgle of talking sounded like a babbling brook. Corbett coughed as his lungs adjusted to the amount of dust that floated through the air. There were two other roads entering the town that were congested with traffic. Corbett turned and looked behind him at the road he had come down. Strange, he thought, not a single soul trailed him. He also thought it odd that he had passed no one on his journey.

He looked at his map once again and made his way through the bustling street. He drove his wagon slowly, along the busy dirt road. A few people yelled at him as his wagon brushed against their market stalls. He neared the edge of town and continued to follow the road, keeping an eye on his map. He hoped he would be out of the busy streets soon. The traffic on the road thinned and went down a small hill, curving and disappearing through a closed gate and back into the forest.

Corbett pulled out the map again to make sure he was going the correct direction. The map showed that William's house sat near the edge of the forest, just a little to the right of the closed gate. Corbett folded the map, scanned his surroundings, and spotted William's house. It looked large from a distance, and it sat alone near the edge of the forest. He wondered why no other houses were around. The land looked beautiful. Maybe William owned the land for the mill. Corbett could see the mill a short distance from the home as he made his way down the road. It sat close to a large foaming river. Corbett wondered if it was the same river he had thrown the mysterious sword into. He worried only for a moment that the sword would somehow mysteriously come floating down it and then shook his head, dismissing the impossible thought. He pulled his wagon to a halt as he arrived at William's home.

William sat on the porch, eyeing the newcomer suspiciously while smoking a pipe. "I presume you are Corbett?"

"Yes I am. Am I at the right home? I am looking for William."

"Sorry for the cold greeting, but you can never be to careful when you live on the edge of the forest. Yes, you have come to the right home. Welcome, Corbett. It's good to see you again. We were expecting you sooner but know how traveling can go." William walked over to Corbett and reached out his hand.

"It's good to see you, too. It has been quite a few years. Thank you for offering me the job so quickly. It has blessed me greatly knowing that my father's friend will be helping in this next stage of my life. I hope I am as good as my father told you."

"I am sure you will be. I bet you need to stretch your legs a little. If you would like, I will show you where you will be working. It is not too far of a walk. We won't be able to linger too long because my wife, Hadley, is cooking dinner."

"A walk would be nice to get a lay of the land, and I didn't realize I was hungry—dinner will be nice, too."

"Excuse me for a minute." William walked toward two men coming out of a barn. "These are my estate hands, Lucas and Riley. They will take care of your horses and your belongings. You will be living in our guest house, which is near the mill."

It felt good to walk in the spring air. Next to the road, the sound of the river rushed past them. He knew this would be a good place to live, and knowing the river separated him from the dark forest comforted him after yesterday's events.

"How did the ride to Gilleran treat you? I know you came down the less-traveled road. Not many people leave the lush land of Midlion to live in the busy streets of Gilleran."

Corbett waited a moment, gauging if he wanted to relate the strange events that occurred on the hill before entering Gilleran. Not knowing much about William, he didn't want to sound like a scared child retelling a tall tale. He decided William would want to hear about what happened, but he would share a shorter version. "My ride was pretty uneventful except for yesterday. My horses spooked after seeing a man hiding at the edge of the forest, delaying me in getting here by a day. But other than that, it had been a nice ride." Corbett noticed William pause in midstep and then continue walking. They were almost at the door of a quaint cabin.

"Hmm...I have not heard of the man mentioned at the edge of the forest for a long time. It does not bode well for Gilleran when he is sighted."

"You know of the stranger?" Corbett asked with surprise.

"Old prophecies and wives' tales, but there is always a grain of truth to them. We can talk about that later. I don't want to bore you with village nonsense. Let us continue the tour of where you will be living and working."

William opened the door of what looked like a well-loved cabin. The entrance opened into a wide-open area with a small, ornately carved fireplace in the corner. The smell of fresh paint hung in the air.

"What do you think? Will this be an adequate place for you?"

Corbett shook his head in disbelief at the good fortune that had befallen him. His parents would be so proud. He smiled to himself. "Wow, this is incredible. Thank you! It seems so large after sharing a house with my parents, and everything is beautifully carved."

"I am glad you like it. You can keep your horses with mine at the main house if you would like. There is a small pasture to the side here for them also. I will not be charging you to live here. Consider it a gift from me and your father."

"Again, thank you," Corbett said as he grazed his hand over a cedar carved desk. "Did you do all this?"

"Mostly, but your father lived here at one time when he worked for my father. He made many improvements. We still have some time. Would you like to see where you will be working, too?"

"Yes, that would be nice."

The mill was only a short distance from Corbett's new home. The fact that William knew of the stranger he had encountered still tugged on his mind.

"William, I am curious about the hooded man I saw. You mentioned there are some village tales."

"There are a few different versions, but I will tell you the one my father always told me and that his father told him. There is a book concerning these strange village tales in my family that gets passed from generation to generation. It is in my library at the house."

William stopped in front of a large building that sat on the edge of the dark river. "This is the mill. Let's continue this conversation later."

William opened the heavy wooden door into a large room. The only noise that could be heard was the spinning of an old water wheel. Corbett breathed deeply, the smell of sawdust reminding him of his father.

"This is where you will be working. We start work before sunrise with the whistle blow and end a little before the sun starts to set. I don't believe in overworking my men. The quality of the production of my mill is well known around Gilleran for being the best despite not matching the quantity of the only other mill in this area."

"I have never heard of a boss taking such good care of his workers. What is the reason you have this work schedule?" Corbett asked curiously.

"I find that rested and happy workers produce the best products. Plus my crew is willing to cross the river to find interesting types of wood across the river that no one else will log due to the mysteries surrounding the forest. Speaking of the forest, that is another reason we do not work past dark here. It is not safe to do so— remaining indoors is best." William continued walking through the darkened mill in the last rays of twilight and lit a lamp. "This will be the area you will be working in."

Corbett looked at the corner that had been sectioned off of the mill with a small wooden fence. It had a nice workbench, a few tools lined the open cupboards, and a couple stools sat in different areas on the floor. Sawdust covered the floor near an intricately carved piece of wood. "What is this?" Corbett ran his hand over what appeared to be upon closer inspection the start of a wooden rocking horse.

"Remember in the letter I sent you the mention of a project for you?"

"Yes."

"This is the project you will be inheriting. There is a young gentleman that visits our mill frequently that requests interesting carved wooden items. This happens to be my attempt at a wooden rocking horse."

Corbett gazed at the attempt on the rocking horse, his mind already spinning with ways to carve it better. "This looks interesting to me. How do you have time to do the projects plus your regular workload?"

"We have been taking turns as time allows us to complete the projects. He is not demanding. Since we are a smaller operation, his projects tend to take a while. When I received your letter, I instantly thought of you for these special projects."

"Thank you, but really why me? You barely know me," Corbett said, hoping he didn't offend his new boss.

"Your father was the best woodworker I have ever seen, and when we had spoken in the past, he confided in me about your natural talent for wood carving. This is what you will be doing with most of your time. You will also learn the inner workings of the mill, but your main job and responsibility will be the projects. If for some reason you can't keep up with the demands of the projects, the other men will take the simpler woodworking—making a fence, door, window frame, and anything else of that nature."

"I hope I can live up to what my father told you. Is this area over here where I will be working?"

"Yes, I preferred this area of the mill for the projects since it is out of the way in the corner and the two windows look toward the river. Do you have any questions before we go eat dinner?"

"Just one. When can I start working?" The idea of having a job where he could be creative all day long and get paid for it made him extremely happy. He hoped whoever this unusual young man was would be easy to please.

"We don't start work again until Monday. Let's make that your first official day. But if you want to familiarize yourself with the mill, here is your key, and you can go in anytime you prefer. Also I pay once a month at the beginning of the month. As I said before, I will not be charging you to live in your new home, but you will need money for other everyday items."

"I have to admit I was unsure of coming to a new town and basically starting a new life. My dad always talked highly of his times in Gilleran. I loved watching my father on his carpentry projects, but I myself have not had a job where I could test out my skills on a regular basis. Hopefully I will not disappoint you. Do you think that the gentleman will want to do business with me since I am young also?"

"I am almost positive he will want to do business with you. He does have a name, but it escapes me at this moment. I guess I'm getting old." William smiled and chuckled, causing the smoke of his pipe to puff sporadically. "I will have an unhappy wife if we do not get to the main house for dinner soon."

William lit another lantern for Corbett to carry and reached above the main door. He pulled down a nice-looking gun and carried it in his free hand. The beginnings of a dark night stretched out before them in the vastness of the rolling hills. William paused at the edge of the mill and held his lantern up toward the forest. The powerful light from the lantern fell flat against the edge of the forest in an unnatural way.

"The forest you see is enchanted. That I know for sure regardless of what the people in town say. The light I hold should penetrate at least to the river's edge, but it never has at night."

They continued their walk to the main house. Corbett's stomach growled, as he felt suddenly weary from his travels, but he politely listened to the story William weaved as they walked.

"My father told me that at some point in the not-too-distant past, there had been a thriving kingdom in the center of the old forest. The road at the closed gate you probably noticed on your way in connected directly with the road you traveled on today. At that time, Gilleran was no more than a few farms. The people of the Wooded Kingdom traveled to Gilleran and befriended the people here. They eventually traded goods with each other and established a fruitful relationship."

William paused to repack his pipe and stood staring out over the dark rolling hills. "Gilleran's farmers began to build larger buildings, and a few wealthy people from the Wooded Kingdom settled in Gilleran, and a few of Gilleran's farmers settled in the Wooded Kingdom. Both places began to thrive and prosper. As word spread of the prosperity in the area, people from other areas began to trickle in and trade for the unusual white bricks. Then, according to the story my father would tell me, a shadow fell upon Gilleran, and the river that flowed from the Wooded Kingdom ceased to flow abundantly. Rather than go see if their newfound friends in the Wooded Kingdom needed help, the people of Gilleran became afraid that they would lose their wealth."

Corbett thought that perhaps William had forgotten about dinner as they continued to stand in the same spot, but then they began their walk to the main house once again.

William continued his story. "The leaders of Gilleran had been corrupted with the newly found riches and ordered the immediate destruction of the bridge that connected Gilleran to the Wooded Kingdom. A few villagers defied the leaders, refusing to destroy the bridge, saying it had brought blessings to the once small Gilleran. The leaders decided to begin construction on the largest gate in town to separate the town of Gilleran from the Wooded Kingdom. The village leaders ignored the refusals of the concerned townspeople and constructed plans for not only a gate but also the destruction of the bridge. When the construction began on the gate, they destroyed the bridge also, hoping to smash the plans of anyone wanting to leave, but a few people left that day to help the Wooded Kingdom, crossing the sickly, muddy river, which once flowed strongly. They were never seen or heard from again, but in a week's time, the river began to flow again and the strange dark cloud lifted from Gilleran. A hooded man walked out of the forest that day and stood in the center of

Gilleran, soaking wet with a sword on his side and an oaken staff in his hand."

William, enthralled in his story, turned to Corbett and excitedly whispered the next part, not giving Corbett a chance to get a word in. "My father would always whisper the words that according to the story were spoken that day: 'You living behind the locked gate have failed the test. You know of what I speak—those of you who came from my kingdom, the Wooded Kingdom. You shall see. One from here will rise up and become great. Your actions have decided the fate. The Dark Kingdom will rise. The Wooded Kingdom is shaken, and Gilleran will continue to live in fear.' The hooded figure was chased from the town that day, appearing occasionally afterward. Sometimes just standing on the edge of the forest staring. The few times he did enter Gilleran, a building would burn or thunderstorms would appear out of nowhere. From that, many stories have been created, and the people of Gilleran have become a suspicious bunch since then, even though most of them say it is a mere story to scare children from crossing the river."

"That is quite a story. Curious that people don't want to remember; if I grew up here, I would be searching to discover what all of it meant."

They had arrived at William's house just as Corbett's stomach let out another loud growl. "I hope I didn't bore you with my story."

"No, not at all. It is very interesting."

"There the two of you are. I was about to enjoy dinner all by myself. Now stop chitchatting, and go wash up," Hadley said.

Corbett felt a little relieved not to have to continue talking. They both obeyed. After washing, they sat at the wooden table. The fresh bread made Corbett's mouth water. As he reached to grab a piece of the warm bread, he noticed William and his wife bow their heads. He quickly followed suit. His hunger could wait to be satisfied for a few more moments. After a quick blessing for the food, he immediately began eating the fresh bread. He eyed the steaming leg of chicken with delight. He was starving.

"Did you enjoy seeing your new place?" Hadley asked in her delicate voice.

"Yes, I can't wait to get started. I also found the story of the hooded man from the...what was it called?...the Wooded Kingdom very interesting as well." Corbett spoke between finished bites of chicken.

Hadley gave William a sideways smile. "I am glad you like it. We are happy to have you here. Your mother and father would be proud of your decision to come here I am sure. William loves sharing the prophecy of Gilleran. I find it interesting myself, although sometimes it is a little long-winded." Hadley gently patted William's hand. "It has been awhile since that man has been sighted, it's hard to believe it was ever true. You didn't see anything while you traveled here, did you?"

"I did have a strange encounter with a hooded man at the edge of the forest yesterday, and after hearing of Gilleran's hooded man, I believe it may be the same one."

"Interesting. We will have to see what comes of it since something seems to always happen after that man is sighted. William will show you where you will be sleeping tonight. You must be exhausted."

"Thank you for dinner. I do feel a tad weary from my travels." Corbett excused himself from the table and followed William to a nice large bedroom. His things had been arranged on the bed, and a washbasin sat on the dresser.

"Oh, I almost forgot. Don't go to bed yet. I will be right back." William stepped out for a few moments, returning with a book. "You can hold on to this while you are here. I happen to have two copies. This is the book that goes with the story I told you tonight. Enjoy! See you in the morning."

"Thank you, William. I feel quite tired after eating. I will sleep well."

William closed the door behind him. Corbett slipped into his pajamas and washed for the night. He flopped on his bed, and before turning out his lantern, he grabbed the plain-looking book. The back cover was black. He flipped it over, and the front cover was a golden color. Bright white words were etched gracefully across the front cover: *The Kingdom of Shadow and Sun*. It looked interesting. He extinguished the lantern and, still holding the book on his chest, fell into a restful sleep.

3

WORK BEGINS

Corbett had two days to learn many new things, and he absolutely loved it. Today would be the day he would meet the young man William had told him so much about. He had completed the rocking horse, taking that time to familiarize himself with his new working environment. The rocking horse sat in his work area. He gazed at his craftsmanship admiringly, feeling a tad proud with his first project completed. Having so much time to be creative with woodworking made him certain he would love this place. The men had greeted Corbett with a smile and a hearty welcome on his first official day at work. A few of them joked already about him being the project guy but praised him on the quality of craftsmanship exhibited by such a young man on the newly finished rocking horse.

"Corbett, do you feel ready to meet the special patron today?" William inquired, talking loudly over one of the many purring saws.

"Yes, I think so. I feel pretty rested. I must confess though I have been staying up late and reading the book you lent me. It is curious what is contained in those pages. It gives me something to ponder while I work. It makes me wonder if that man I saw that day really is the same prophet from those pages. I think he is, but then I think, *Why me, a stranger to this land?* Like I said, it gives me a lot to ponder."

"That is what I like to hear. Speaking of your special patron, which I again apologize for not remembering his name, I just saw him ride in on his horse. I will wait here to introduce the two of you, then, my young apprentice, you are on your own. Oh, before I forget, try not to stare," William said this with a sly wink.

Before Corbett could ask about William's comment, the young man opened the mill door. The morning sun silhouetted his tall physique, and as the man turned, Corbett noticed a prominent hunch on the man's back under his cloak that seemed uncharacteristic. Corbett could tell the young man commanded a presence of respect despite this misplaced deformity.

The man walked over in a few long, easy strides, stopping beside William. "Good morning, William." He gave William a large slap on the back.

"Good morning. I have good news for you," William said, trying to inconspicuously rub the spot that had just been slapped.

"Really? You finished my latest project. Wow, that has to be some kind of record." He eyed the rocking horse, suddenly noticing a muscular young man standing next to it.

"Actually, I did not do the entire project myself. I would like to introduce you to my godson, Corbett. He is going to be the one working with you from now on. His father was a renowned carpenter in his younger days before an unfortunate accident made him change careers. Corbett, this is your new customer…" The name suddenly dawned on William. "Oh, yes, Dem. That's right."

It took Corbett a split second to respond. He had not known that William considered him a godson. Also he had never known why his father stopped being a carpenter, something he loved to do, to become a hard-working farmer. He had always thought he switched careers to be closer to his mother's family. He would have to remember to ask William about those things later. Corbett reached out his hand and strongly shook Dem's large hand. A small shock transferred between their hands.

Dem narrowed his eyes for a moment at Corbett and then broke into a huge grin. "An electrifying greeting on the first meeting has to mean great things. I'm sure we will have much fun working together." Dem slapped Corbett on his muscular, lean back and was shocked once again. "Not sure what to think about all this static electricity. Must be the weather. But something I do know is that the rocking horse is magnificent."

Dem walked into Corbett's workspace and ran his hand over the white spotted rocking horse, his fingers pausing on the individually carved eyelashes and the lifelike eyes. "Corbett, I see great things in our future. Here is the payment for the horse." He picked up the horse and walked toward the door. "I will be right back. I have a drawing of my next project for you."

"Corbett, I think you have this handled. Sorry for springing the godson thing on you. In the midst of everything this morning, I forgot to ask. You don't have to be our godson if you don't want to, but we would be honored. We loved your parents."

"Wow, yes, I am honored to be your godson. I will also have to ask you later about the accident you mentioned. My father never shared that with me."

"Hmm...yes, the accident. It is still a painful memory for me. It looks like we have a few moments before Dem returns. I am to blame—it is simple really."

"You are?" Corbett asked in shock.

"Yes, my inattention to safety led to a large piece of wood to propel off a saw into a flat of logs, causing them to fall into the area your father worked. Your father tried to get out of the way, but a log heavily grazed the side of his head, leaving him to have poor vision and an unstable hand on that side. It took me a long time not to feel guilty. Your father graciously forgave me long before I forgave myself. Hope that clears things up for you."

"I always wondered what happened. He never spoke of it, and, yes, it is nice to finally know what happened after all these years. Thank you for telling me."

"You're welcome. I will leave you to your new project coming in the door. If you have any more questions about the accident, feel free to ask me later. Have fun!" William patted Corbett's back with a thoughtful smile on his face as he walked away.

"Corbett, here is my newest creation." On Corbett's workbench, Dem quickly laid out a few ink drawings etched into thick paper, talking to him like they had known each other for a lifetime.

"These drawings are a little confusing. Are these plans for wooden lanterns? Won't they catch on fire if you put a candle in them?" Corbett continued to stare at the drawings, afraid that he had already offended his new customer. The mill seemed quiet as he waited for a response. Sometimes his honesty came out before he could think about it.

"Nobody has ever critiqued my drawings before. I knew I would like you." He elbowed Corbett in the side. "You are correct. They are four matching wooden lanterns. I will be putting the finishing of clear blown glass from my kingd...I mean village in them when I return home.

"I have not seen such a design before, but I am pretty sure I can make something close to this. Are they a gift for someone?"

"They are a gift for my wife to fill with fireflies in the warm summer evenings. Feel free to add what you will to the lanterns. I am excited to see your creative workmanship."

"Fireflies, what a unique idea. This will be fun to create." Corbett grabbed a pencil and began making notes on the drawings.

"Corbett, I must run. Thank you again, and I look forward to our next meeting. In the past, the other men I worked with were never quite sure when a project would be completed. Do you have any idea how long four lanterns will take you?"

Corbett eyed the drawings, inspecting, holding them up, and twisting them a couple different ways. "I would say give me one week from today, and I can have all of them completed. I am looking forward to challenging my current skills."

"Thanks, Corbett. I will see you in a week." Dem walked toward the door, stopped to visit with William, glanced a few times at Corbett, and then sauntered out the door.

Corbett watched Dem gallop away on his magnificent white steed as he held the rocking horse rather awkwardly in his lap. Corbett smiled to himself. Even though he had just met Dem, he could tell they would soon be friends. That shock that had passed between their hands felt like more than just static electricity—almost like something was telling the both of them to pay attention to this moment. Corbett turned his attention to the lantern drawings, grabbed a pencil, and began adding a few more things to the sketches. After a while, he stood back to admire his drawings. He had added four fireflies flying down one side of each lantern. Then the delicate sides that would house the glass, he designed to look like four tree branches. The top of each lantern was the shape of a flowering lily pad with hidden holes for breathing. Each lantern would also be easily carried with a handle that would be two intertwined tree branches. He couldn't wait to get started. The bell rang for lunch.

"Come on, Corbett. Let's eat," one of the men shouted.

Corbett sighed, not wanting to wait another minute to get started but set aside his drawings and began the walk with the other men to the main house. The week passed quickly as Corbett diligently worked on the lantern project, stopping only to eat, sleep, and occasionally read the book he had borrowed. He never again discussed his father's accident with William. Finally having the knowledge of what actually happened comforted him in a way.

Corbett had his back to the door, putting the finishing touches on the lanterns. His mind was so focused he heard nothing around him, including Dem entering the mill.

"Good morning, Corbett," Dem said loudly.

Corbett jumped and turned. "Sorry, I didn't hear you enter the mill. Your projects are finished. I can't believe it has been a week already. Time really does move fast sometimes. Four of them are in the wooden box there near where you are standing, and the fifth one here I am almost done with."

Dem noticed the wooden box near his feet. He opened the heavy lid carefully, and four beautifully carved lily pads greeted his eyes. *The empty space in the very center must be for the fifth lantern*, he thought. "Wait, Corbett, did you say five lanterns were made? I only drew plans for four."

Corbett turned around, and in his hand, he held a wooden lantern not like the rest. Carved out of a white wood, it almost seemed to glimmer in his hands. "I hope you don't mind. After finishing the four, I had an idea for one more. The wood across the river is unique and worked better than I expected for this fifth one."

"Mind? Never. This is amazing." Dem took the delicate yet sturdy white lantern out of Corbett's hands and gazed at it. The white bark, when inspected closely and held to the sunlight, had fireflies etched into its sides. The top lily pad flower had been painted a faint pink, and the leaves had a slight dusting of green. When Dem lifted the lid of the lantern and peered inside, a small carving of a frog greeted his curious eyes. He set it lightly in the center of the carefully packed wooden box. The other men of the mill had also wandered over.

"Corbett, I am at a loss for what to say. But having not known you that long, I would have to say..." Dem reached over the railing that separated him and Corbett and patted him heavily on the back. "Thank you. My wife will be eternally grateful. You have provided me with the best birthday gift ever."

The men in the mill were also mesmerized by the craftsmanship that Corbett had created. It seemed almost otherworldly, and from that moment forward, his skills continued to grow and so did the friendship between him and Dem.

The year passed quickly as he established himself in Gilleran. On one of his many front porch chats with William, he met a wonderful, feisty girl named Ida, who cleaned William's home as well as other homes in town. He smiled to himself as he remembered the fond look on William's face as Ida and Corbett were first introduced. He found time to get to know Ida and her fiery yet quirky personality as he met her on different occasions working for William. The first thing he remembered learning about her was that she worked hard and sent most of her money to her mother, who had a large debt to pay off after her husband had passed away suddenly. And as time would have it, Corbett and Ida fell in love. Their courtship was blissful, and they planned on getting married one day but wanted to be able to be more financially secure. They decided to wait a few more years and perhaps buy, or preferably build, a house big enough near William to house not only them but also Ida's mother. As they saved and worked, another happy year passed.

William made it a point to celebrate his employees' work anniversaries by giving them the day off. He had done this for Corbett two times, which meant, as the third anniversary approached, he would have yet another day off. This time William was going to do something different. As a gift, William gave Corbett a week since he had not missed a single day of work in his three years of working. Corbett couldn't believe he had worked for William for three years already.

"Has it really been three years? It doesn't seem like it. I feel as if I started here as a young boy. Where has the time gone? So much has happened in the past few years. It flew by, I guess."

"It is hard to imagine that three years ago you were just learning the ropes around here. I look at you not only as a seasoned employee but a mature young man. What do you think you will do with your week off?" William asked Corbett as they walked back from the mill, ending another good day of work.

"I planned on spending the week with my wonderful girlfriend, but she will be out of town taking care of a few family matters with her mother. Her mother's boss is once again refusing to pay her."

"Wow, I hope Ida's mother will be able to get out of that situation soon. I assume you told her you wanted to go. I bet I know how that went. She is a feisty and stubborn one that one but such a sweet young lady at the same time."

"You know her well." Corbett smiled. "I told her I could go with her, but she insisted that she would rather I go do something fun since it is my three-year work anniversary. Such a frustrating thing to deal with, but she continually amazes me every day as I get to know her more. The wisdom she has shown during this tricky time in her mother's life has been amazing to watch."

"Ida is a very special young woman. You two are perfect for each other. If you are not spending the week with her, what will you be doing?"

"Of course, I happened to mention all of this to Dem, what Ida would be doing during my work anniversary, because I confide in him almost as much as I confide in you. I will be traveling with Dem to his village and meeting his family. Looks like no rest for me during my break."

"Rest, who needs rest when there are new people to meet and places to go?" William said this with a fatherly smile.

"Yes, I guess I can rest another time. I am not sure what to expect. Dem and I have become good friends over the past few years, so this will be nice to finally see the different things he has told me about." Corbett had just reached the steps of his house.

"Have a good time. I will see you when you return. I am sure it will be an adventure spending a week with Dem. Enjoy yourself. You deserve it." William patted Corbett on the back as he said good-bye.

Corbett noticed William looked a little sad, but maybe he was just imagining things.

Corbett shut and locked the door behind him. The last remaining rays of light flittered through the window, causing his living room to have a soft orange glow. He sighed—he really did enjoy living here. Three years. He was now twenty. Wow, so much had happened to him, he felt like a man compared to the boy he was when he first arrived. He lit a few lanterns and began packing for his trip.

4

UNEXPECTED

"What is that noise?" Corbett said to himself groggily as he lifted his head. It felt as if he had fallen asleep only moments ago. He laid his head back down. Again a loud knock came from his front door. He got up, reluctantly peeking out of his drawn window curtain, the sky barely lit with the early morning sun. He dropped his head and sighed. No sleeping in on his first day off. Dem had arrived. Dem was dressed nicely and holding what looked like an amazing breakfast.

On seeing Corbett's face through the window, Dem burst through the front door. "Good morning, Corbett! I apologize that I arrived early, but I wanted to get an early start to our fun weekend." Dem waltzed into Corbett's quaint sitting room and plopped breakfast haphazardly on the table.

"I guess I should say good morning. I am not quite awake. Make yourself comfortable..." Before Corbett could finish his sentence, Dem was already lighting a fire.

"It feels a little chilly in here. Please take your time getting ready."

Dem perused the few pictures on the wall. He had never been in Corbett's home. For being a quaint house, it had well-made furnishings, no doubt Corbett's masterful handiwork. Dem picked up a black-and-white portrait of what must have been Corbett's parents. He wondered how long it would take Corbett to get ready. He wanted some of the breakfast he had brought but decided to wait for his friend. Dem looked over a small bookshelf and found an interesting book. He sat in the rocking chair near the fire and began reading *The Kingdom of Shadow and Sun*. The book looked familiar. It stirred a memory of his father reading to him. Was this the same book? No, it couldn't be. He was so enthralled in his reading, he didn't notice Corbett standing next to him. He mouthed the sentence silently: "Buildings rise and buildings fall. Kingdoms rise and fall..." He jumped suddenly, noticing Corbett.

"Sorry, this book is fascinating. Do you mind if I borrow it while you are with me this week? It reminds me of a book my father used to read to my brother and me. I think it might be the same one, which is odd, since I always thought ours was a collection of stories passed down by our family members."

"That is odd, no I don't mind if you bring the book. It will be interesting to see if it is the same book."

They both walked over to the table and grabbed a plate, filling it with fresh fruit. "Did you read the part in the book where it is talking about kingdoms rising and falling?" Dem asked between bites of a biscuit covered in strawberries.

"Yes. For some reason, that little verse, if that is what you want to call it, stuck in my head. Kind of like a sad memory. Don't know why, but what it is saying is true. Kingdom's do rise and fall. Makes me think of how the sun rises and sets, allowing night to rise. I guess to me it alludes to the struggle between light and dark. I didn't get far in the book because I started to think about it all."

"I can see that. It will be a good discussion for our ride to my home. Let's clean quickly so we can leave. Are you are ready?"

"I am ready." Corbett helped Dem clean and pack what was left of the food. He quickly scanned the house, making sure everything was in order.

While they had been eating, the men who had also arrived with Dem had gotten Corbett's horse Titian ready to ride and already stored his things on one of the packhorses.

Climbing on his copper steed, Corbett sighed. "Wow, I could get used to this. It is always so much work to get a horse ready. Thank you very much." He looked in the direction of the regally dressed man who sat on top of a beautiful white horse. He nodded courteously.

"I agree, it is nice. Come ride next to me. We will ride and talk until the trail forces us to ride single file."

They talked for such a long time, lost in conversation about the book, that Corbett didn't notice the narrowing of the trail and the darkening of the sky. One of the men with them, whose name Corbett still did not know, rode quietly behind them. When he spoke, it startled both of them.

"Excuse me, sirs, but we should stop here for the night," he said with a rich, warm voice.

"That ride went faster than I can ever remember it going. Thank you, Derek, It slipped my mind this morning, Corbett. Let me introduce you to my estate hand, Derek." They rode the horses to a nearby stream just off the narrowing trail. They worked together to make a little dinner and set up a few cots under the open, twinkling sky. In the morning, Corbett woke feeling refreshed. Waking up to the smell of ham and eggs cooking over an open flame also awakened his stomach.

"Good morning. Derek, right?"

"Good morning, sir. Yes, Derek is right."

"Where is Dem?"

"He is sleeping on the other side of the horses over there." Derek pointed to a little grove of trees. Corbett could see Dem between the horses, lying on a cot.

"Should we wake him, do you think?"

"Ha, I think we will wait till the sun has fully risen. Then we can wake him, but the smell of breakfast usually gets him up." Derek handed a plate of sizzling ham and fried eggs to Corbett.

"This tastes amazing. Thank you. If you don't mind me asking, how long have you helped Dem?"

"That is a fair question. Since he was a small lad. I have known him and his family for many years."

Corbett thought that could not be true because Derek did not look any older than either Dem or himself. But all that came out between mouthfuls was, "Oh. Hey, look, you were right." Dem had woken and was walking toward them with his usually mischievous grin.

"Good morning to the two of you. What a delicious-smelling breakfast. Thank you, Derek. We should reach my home by nightfall. We will stop briefly for lunch. Do you miss Ida?" Dem said with a knowing grin.

Corbett thought this was an odd question to ask so early in the morning. "I guess so. But I am happy for the opportunity to finally get to know my best friend a little better. Why do you ask?"

"Oh, you only mentioned her name about five times in your sleep." He gently jabbed Corbett in the ribs and chuckled along with Derek.

Corbett's face turned a little red, but he laughed with them. "I guess with trying to figure out the best time to get married, she is on my mind a lot. Is that why you slept by the horses?"

Dem just smiled and stood. Derek had already cleaned and was getting the horses ready.

"Jeez, how in the world does Derek move so fast?"

"That, my friend, is a mystery even to me. Ready to ride?"

The three of them left the campsite. When the sun was at its highest, they stopped briefly for a small meal. Then they were on their way.

Corbett didn't know how much farther he could ride; his legs ached. The sun had set, and the moon began to rise as they crested another hill on the path, which had widened and become an old cobblestone road. As they paused on the hill, Corbett wearily gazed before him. A sparkling village of little lights greeted his eyes. The road wound down until it stopped at an enormous white palace with waterfalls on either side, and then it rounded a bend and was lost in the darkness of the night.

"Wow, I have never set foot in an actual kingdom before. So strange that a beautiful place like this is so close to me, and yet I have never heard of it. Who is the king?"

"This is my home. I am happy to hear you think it's beautiful. We are almost to my house, and then we will talk more but probably not much tonight since we are tired from our journey."

As Dem spoke, Corbett noticed just a hint of change in his voice, just a little more commanding than friendly. He also realized as they rode down the hill that Dem had not answered his question. He figured that was because they were all so tired from their little journey.

They rode by quaint little homes with flickering lanterns in the windows. Many shops dotted the town with their intricately carved wooden signs. Corbett recognized his handiwork throughout the village, and it made him feel honored that his things graced such a beautiful place. They rode until the road curved around the brightly lit palace. Dem and Derek got off their horses, and the castle door opened. A few more people came out and took the horses, stopping at Corbett's horse, as he still sat on top of the tired steed. Corbett was staring, his mouth hanging slightly open. A beautiful woman with long dark hair ran and greeted Dem. Corbett also noticed a sulky-looking fellow who looked similar to Dem. He did not greet anyone.

"Umm...sir, excuse me, but we will take your horse for the night."

"Oh, why, yes, I am so sorry. I am tired and to be honest a little mesmerized by the sight before me. I have never seen such things before."

Corbett stiffly got off his horse and walked toward Dem with hundreds of thoughts floating through his tired head. Maybe Dem was a favored servant or maybe a grandchild of the king that lived here, or maybe this beautiful woman was the king's daughter and she had fallen in love with Dem. He stopped just short of the embracing, smiling couple. All the tiredness seemed to have disappeared from Dem's face.

"What do you think, Corbett?"

"I think I am impressed but wondering why you never mentioned any of this before. Who are you, Dem?"

"Well," Dem said as he put his arm around his friend's shoulder, and they faced the inviting palace. "This is my beautiful home. This is my wife, Juliana. I am the king of this kingdom, and I am not exactly misshapen on my back."

"What do you mean not exactly misshapen? I thought you were born with a deformity."

Dem took off his long coat and unfurled a pair of large white wings as Corbett stared, trying to process the sights before him.

Corbett looked squarely in his friend's face, squinting to make sure all of this was not an elaborate joke.

Trying to deal with the shock of what his friend was showing him. "If all you say is true, Dem, then why haven't you revealed any of this to me sooner?"

"I wanted a true friend who happened to be normal and live a normal life. I didn't think it would ever happen until that day we met and that shock passed between our hands. I remembered Juliana mentioning something about that a while ago. It made me take notice of the moment a little more than I normally would, and then you and I clicked, kind of like brothers should. I hide my wings because people of your town are not as accepting as they once were. I hope you will forgive me for not sharing this part of my life with you."

"Of course I forgive you. I guess I am just in awe and maybe a little shock; the wings will take some getting used to. Wow is all I can say. It's nice to meet you, Juliana." He shook her warm, dainty hand.

She gave him a big hug. "It is great to finally meet the friend of Dem's I have heard so much about. I have fallen in love with your woodworking. Dem may have forgotten to mention this, but he said a shock passed between the two of you when you met. My grandmother used to tell me an old myth that if such a thing ever happened to two people at the same time that would mean they were both destined for greatness. And that their paths would always be connected somehow. I always wondered if I would ever meet anyone that had that happen and now I have. See, you were meant to come here. Oh, I chatter too much. It has been so long since we have had a guest. Please follow us to the castle."

"Thank you, Juliana, for sharing. I don't think of it as chatter at all. It is very interesting in fact."

The three walked up the white marble stairs into the majestic palace. The same sulky man he noticed earlier still stood near the doorway.

Dem walked up to him, threw his arm around his shoulder, and jostled him a bit, grinning. The other man did not look impressed. "This is my younger brother, Irenen. Irenen, this is my amazingly talented wood-working friend, Corbett."

Irenen extended his hand out of obligation and shook Corbett's hand loosely.

A sharp shiver coursed through Corbett's body. "Sorry, I must have gotten chilled from the night. Nice to meet the brother of my friend."

Irenen stared at him a moment before he spoke in a flat voice that sounded too old for the young body it came out of. "Welcome to the kingdom. Enjoy your stay." Then he walked outside into the night.

"You will have to excuse my brother. He is not the happiest fellow. I am amazed he spoke to you."

"Oh, I just figured your brother was tired. We did probably wake him."

"You are always so kind. I am feeling rather exhausted. Your room is already prepared. My servant Alex will show you the way. Juliana and I will meet you in the morning for breakfast."

Corbett obediently followed the young woman, Alex, through a few hallways until they stopped at a dark wood door.

"This is where you will be staying while you are here. Someone will come wake you for breakfast." Alex pushed the door open and left Corbett standing alone in the unfamiliar room.

A small fire burned in a stone fireplace that had carvings of trees on the side. A sitting chair with a footstool sat near the fire. A large bed with thick red blankets sat opposite the fireplace. Corbett flopped himself down in the overstuffed royal-blue chair. The fire warming his sleepy body, he kicked off his boots and reclined in the chair. He quickly fell asleep.

He awoke in the morning, and sitting up quickly, he wondered how he had gotten into the bed. The early morning sun streamed in through an open window, and a breeze lightly blew the curtains draped along its sides. A set of his clean clothes lay on the chair near the now dead fire. He washed his face in a decorative blue water bowl in his room. His growling stomach could be ignored no longer. As he opened the door, Derek greeted him.

"Good morning, sir. I hope you don't mind, but when I checked on you last night, I moved you to the more comfortable bed. I see you found your clean clothes." Derek chuckled out loud. "I can also hear that you are hungry. If you would, please follow me."

"Oh, I don't mind."

They walked through the castle at a brisk pace and arrived at the dining hall. Dem and Juliana already sat giggling with each other at a rather small table for such a large and grand dining room.

"Good morning, Corbett. Derek told me you fell asleep in the sitting chair. It is a rather comfortable place, I agree. That used to be my room as a child. Here, come sit by us." Dem patted the seat next to him.

After Corbett sat, the doors to what must have been the kitchen opened, and servants carrying plates of fresh fruit and sizzling ham and biscuits slathered in some type of sauce entered the room. The plates were placed before the three of them, the delicious aroma tickling all of their noses.

All three put a moderate amount of food on their plates. The servants poured fresh-squeezed juice, and Corbett let the delicious food melt in his mouth. He closed his eyes for a moment, soaking in the warmth of the morning sun. When he opened them, a drawing lay beside his plate. He picked it up and examined it. The sketching and handwriting were unmistakable. Dem had just handed him a new project. He looked at Dem.

"What do you think?" Dem asked with a silly grin while Juliana leaned over, smiling in his direction.

Corbett looked at the drawing as he took another bite of a steaming, buttery biscuit. It looked to be a table but not just any table—a really large table. The number twenty-four lightly lined the two longer sides of the table. Whimsical drawings of birds were sprawled randomly across the page with arrows pointing to the different legs of the table. A masterfully drawn oak tree graced one of the corners of the paper with the word "center" written by it. Dem stared intently at Corbett's face as he concentrated on the drawing.

Corbett looked up, thinking Dem had to be joking. "Did I read this right? A table to fit forty-eight people? Are you aware of how much lumber that will take? Not to mention the man-hours it is going to take me to build it if you are serious? I would ask you what you need it for, but I know you would give me some riddle of an answer."

"I need it for me to sit at of course." Dem smiled. "Don't worry about the details. I have that all taken care of. The lumber is here already, in a workshop I set up in one of the seldom-used stables. If you are willing to do the project, you can stay here at the palace instead of commuting back and forth."

"What will I tell William if I say yes to this?"

"I have already spoken with William about needing you closer at hand if you accept the offer. He did hesitate at the offer, but after we talked awhile, he agreed it would be a good opportunity for you as long as he can still attend your wedding whenever you and Ida finally pick a date."

"I don't know what to say," Corbett said in shock at what Dem was suggesting.

"I will be able to pay you rather handsomely. I thought it would take some time for you to build, and the transportation of a table that large would be impossible. Having you stay with me only seemed logical. Ida could move here also."

Juliana put a light hand on her husband and said, "Please, Corbett, if you want to take some time to think about this..."

Corbett's heart pounded as he stared into Juliana's face. What had he done to have such fortune shine upon him? What an amazing opportunity. He looked down at the table a moment as his thoughts drifted to William and the mill. William and his wife were the closest thing to family he had, not to mention all his friends at the mill. He would miss all of them dearly but felt comforted that if any of them chose, they could visit. This place was really not that far away. He didn't need to relocate Ida until after their wedding. He would be able to journey home a few times he was sure.

"I do not need time to think about such a wonderful opportunity. I feel honored that you would consider having me in your kingdom. Thank you for talking to William."

"You're welcome. I knew that if you were going to say yes that would be one of the things that would make you hesitate. I also hoped that asking William would not offend you."

"Offended, no. You were right though: William's lack of approval of this would have been the only thing that held me back. About the table, of course I can build that for you," Corbett said with a large smile.

"Welcome, then, to your new home." Dem patted Corbett on the back.

"Thank you. I look forward to living here. I guess Ida could help, but if it is all the same to you, I would rather her stay at William's until our wedding unless she really wants to come with me. I think it would be best for her since she still travels back and forth to assist her mother."

"That is fine with us, but if you happen to change your mind about Ida, it is OK. We would be happy to have your family here. Here is three months' pay up front for you to give to Ida. It might help her decide to come with you." He slid an envelope that contained the money into Corbett's hand. "You won't have to worry about her being taken care of if she decides to stay in Gilleran. She will be joining you here before you know it when you get married. You are the most talented woodworker I know." Dem reached out his gloved hand for an agreement shake.

Corbett hesitated for a moment. What would he tell his girlfriend so she would understand? He would come up with something. "Dem, your requests never cease to amaze me. I will agree to build you this table as long as I do have some time to see Ida if she stays behind." Corbett reached out and shook Dem's gloved hand.

"Thank you," Juliana and Dem said simultaneously.

"If you two would excuse me, I have some things I need to do. Thank you again. I can't wait to have a table to fit all our friends and family around." Juliana gracefully exited the room.

"Would you like to see where you will be working?" Dem inquired.

"Sure. I still can't believe the project you want me to build. It will be incredible when it is finished. I promise."

"I know it will. That is why I chose you. Here, follow me."

They walked to the end of the large dining hall where two doors stood. Dem pushed them open, and a large workshop greeted Corbett's eyes. It was fitted with the finest tools he had ever seen. He ran his hands over a few of the workbenches. Light streamed in through numerous windows from high above.

"This is beautiful. I will love working here." He stopped and stared at three rather large piles of different kinds of lumber. "I don't recognize most of this wood, but I am willing to try anything. I should study the drawing first and get my affairs in order. I know I just arrived, but can I leave by tomorrow? The sooner I can start on the project, the faster I can finish. Only if that is OK with you. If you give me the directions, I can ride by myself."

"I don't mind at all. That will give me some time to get your living quarters ready, which I almost forgot to show you." He moved through the brightly lit shop and opened the only other door at the front of the building. It opened into a beautiful living area.

"I am thrilled that you want to build the table for us. Thank you for being my friend even though I didn't really tell you everything about me."

"Don't worry. You are more than a friend. I consider you family, and learning more about you, even if it is different, is helpful for our friendship."

"As always you are too kind. If you still want to leave quickly, you can leave in the morning. I will have Derek ride with you. It would ease my mind knowing you are not alone in an unfamiliar forest. He will stay in town until you are ready to leave. Thank you, friend." Dem patted Corbett on the back again and walked out the front doors.

Corbett felt an unexplained shiver creep into his skin. He noticed the king's brother briskly walking away from the corner of the room. Such an odd fellow, Corbett thought. The day passed quickly, and before he knew it, he was already waking up to an early morning. He dressed quickly, not wanting Derek to wait for him. He jumped on his horse, and they began the ride to Gilleran.

Dem held Juliana as they watched from their bedroom window.

"Do you think he will like it here?" Juliana asked.

"I do. I don't know how he will live without Ida if she decides not to come. I know I couldn't have lived that far away from you while we were dating. We will have to make sure he gets adequate time to see her, and soon she will join him."

They watched until Derek and Corbett disappeared out of view.

5

THE QUESTION

Corbett took Derek to a local inn until he could get his affairs in order. He rode slowly to his quaint home by the mill, where Ida probably awaited his return. She stayed at William's home but spent as much time as she could in Corbett's home. Once they were married, she would officially move in. For the moment, the arrangement worked, although every night he walked her to William's door, the two of them felt sad even though they were only apart for the night. It suddenly dawned on him why William's expression had seemed sad the day before he left for Dem's home. William and his wife would miss Ida and Corbett greatly. It comforted him knowing that Dem had already spoken to William and that he could visit as often as he was able.

Corbett's thoughts shifted back to Ida. What would he tell her? How would he tell her? He finally figured out what to tell Ida as he entered the front door. Hopefully she had returned from her trip. He instantly knew Ida was home because the small dinner table had dinner waiting for him. He never could figure out how she always seemed to know when he would be there for dinner. She always told him it was just a feeling. The smell of fresh bread greeted his nose. Ida came around the corner and greeted Corbett with a big hug. She looked into Corbett's eyes with her fiery green eyes.

"I am so happy to see you. I missed you."

"Oh, I missed you, too. Did you have a good time?"

"I did have a good time with my mother. I wish she wanted to leave that area though. It would make things so much easier. But I can understand. She has good memories in that town, except for those of her boss. Our wedding can't come soon enough." Ida stepped back and saw an unusual sadness in Corbett's eyes. "Did something happen while you were at Dem's village?"

"I had hoped to tell you after dinner, but if you want, we can talk."

"Please, dinner can wait. I want to know what has happened to my joyful Corbett."

Corbett swallowed, hoping she would understand what he was about to share. "There is a new job opportunity for me. There is no easy way to say this, but my talents are required at Dem's village, which is a long day's ride from here. They want me to leave as soon as possible. I have been paid handsomely in advance for my agreement to help." Ida sat silently waiting for Corbett to continue. "I know we usually talk these things over first, but I just took the opportunity. We need more money, and it will only be for a few months. It will help us pay off the debt that your mother still owes her employer, and then we can get married with no more money obligations, and easing both our minds about your mother's well-being will be nice, too. I will come see you a few times. I promise." He held Ida's hands and stared at her face, trying to gauge her reaction.

She let a few tears slip from her eyes and gave Corbett a huge hug. "Oh, Corbett, I will miss you. I understand this is an incredible opportunity for both of us. I sure will miss you though. You promise you will come see your lonely girlfriend. If you don't, I will come find you," Ida said with a fiery look.

"Of course I will, and if it all works out, perhaps we can both relocate there. Don't worry, you won't have to come find me. I can't stand being that long without you."

Corbett and Ida embraced and lingered. Corbett wiped away Ida's tears. He gently grabbed her by the waist and walked with her into the kitchen. They both sat together at the small dining room table. They said an evening prayer and began eating.

"Oh, I almost forgot. Here is the money." He pulled the thick envelope from his pocket. "They said it was at least three months' worth of wages." Corbett slid the money across the table, still feeling a bit weepy.

"Oh, honey. Thank you. I still can't believe another mill has heard about your woodworking ability, but it is not surprising considering how much Dem works with you. You two are close friends anyway. It is probably because of all those amazing things you make for Dem. I would tell the world of your talents if I had the means to." Ida said this talking fast, trying to hide her emotions.

Ida opened the envelope and gasped. At least a year's worth of wages working for William lay inside the envelope. "How many months will you be gone?"

"Only three months at the most," Corbett said as he took a bite of the roasted beef and potatoes. "Why? Is there not enough money?"

"Umm...here. You look." Ida slid the envelope back to Corbett, still in disbelief.

Corbett began counting and then counted again. "I was told I would be paid handsomely in advance. I guess this is what they meant. Unbelievable."

"A blessing in the midst of our sadness," remarked Ida. "This is more than enough for us; we can pay off my mother's debt and get her a nice place to live, too."

"Yes, it is," Corbett said with a nervous grin, an idea stirring in him.

Ida and Corbett finished their dinner. Ida left the cleaning for the next day. She wanted to spend as much time with Corbett as possible before he left. She helped him pack and get the horse ready so he could leave in the morning. Then Corbett walked her in the cool night to William's house, and they parted ways on the front porch step. Both of them drifted off into a comfortable yet sad sleep.

In the morning, Corbett ate a small breakfast with Ida, who had come early in the morning to see that he didn't leave anything important behind. She went out to the barn and helped him with his things.

"I love you, Ida," Corbett said, hugging her tightly. He had rethought his decision to not bring her and had already done many things before she woke. Still hugging Ida lightly, he whispered, "Marry me, Ida." Her breath caught in surprise. "I can't live without you."

Derek walked around the corner of the barn with a beautiful horse ready to ride. Three horses in total stood before Ida's blurry eyes.

"I love you, Corbett, but the debt, my mother—"

"I have taken care of it, my dear. We ride to our home today if you still want to marry me," Corbett said with a smile.

"Still? Are you crazy? Of course I will marry you!" Ida hugged Corbett tightly around the neck.

"Oh, Ida, I love you. Everything is ready to go. Grab whatever you need for today, and let us be off to our new life together. What do you think about having a wedding next week?" he asked hesitantly, not knowing how she would respond.

"Yes, let's move the wedding. What about William, Hadley, your friends at the mill—"

"I already surprised William and Hadley with an early visit this morning. They are coming early next week to help us with anything we need. Oh, Ida, you are going to absolutely love where we are going. More surprises await you there. Hurry, go get ready. We want to start this adventure sooner rather than later, right?"

"Oh, of course, Corbett," Ida said, kissing him fiercely on the cheek. She hurried to William's house and grabbed what few belongings she had, her mind spinning with excitement. She couldn't believe it. She was about to start a new life with the love of her life. She emerged quickly, the sun shining brightly on her beaming face, her red hair glistening in the morning rays.

Corbett sat atop his horse, gazing lovingly at his future bride. She looked elegant in the morning light, her red hair matching her fiery personality that he loved. Her beautiful steed, a gift from Dem, awaited her. William and Hadley stood on the front porch, hugging Ida.

"We will miss you two, and we love you both. You have become family to us. We look forward to helping you with the wedding and can't wait until we come in a few days with your mother. Ride safe and start enjoying your new life with the joy that is always bubbling out of you," Hadley said with happy tears slipping down her cheeks.

William and Hadley hugged Ida one more time, and then she walked over to the horse that awaited her.

"Ida, you look beautiful."

"Thank you, Corbett. It's only because you love me so much," she said with a big grin.

"This is Derek. He works for Dem."

"Hello, and nice to meet you," Ida said as Derek assisted her in getting onto the large white steed.

As they neared the edge of William's land and were about ride out of view, Corbett heard his name being shouted. He looked in the direction of the voice, or was that voices? Over the hill came the entire crew from the mill with William leading the way.

"Honey, why don't you ride out to greet all of them? Take all the time you need. I will wait here with Derek.

Who knows, they might have some new marital advice for you," Ida said with a wink.

Corbett rode to meet the boisterous group. Each man carried a gift. Seeing all his old friends brought tears to Corbett's eyes. He jumped off his horse, and though he had just seen William, he gave him another hug and greeted all of his friends.

"We know you are getting ready to leave, but we couldn't let you go without thanking you for your time here. You know we consider you our son. I know we will be visiting you soon with the upcoming wedding, but a few others wanted to say congratulations."

At that moment, all the men started to pat Corbett on the back as they handed them their gifts. They picked him up on their shoulders shouting, "To ancient times and distant music, may your new life bring you great fortune." They jostled each other around for a bit. Some said they would try to make the wedding. Others wished Corbett happiness. Work would prevent most of them from coming since they wanted to make sure William and his wife could attend for an extended period of time. Having no children of their own, this was their opportunity to dote on their godson and soon-to-be daughter-in-law. Corbett appreciated the men sacrificing their time off to allow William and Hadley to attend. He would miss all of them.

"I knew you were destined for incredible things before you came to work here. I think this will be another great adventure in your life journey."

"Thank you, William. I'm really going to miss it here. I hope I am making the right decision."

"You are. Your parents would be proud. I have traveled to the Wooded Kingdom a few times, searching for things from that book I gave you to read, which is officially yours. It is an incredibly mysterious land."

"I will treasure that book and look forward to seeing you very soon."

"I can't wait to join you in your celebration next week. We will really miss you around here though. We will have to visit often." William gave Corbett another big hug. "We have kept you long enough. Go start your adventure together. We will see you next week." William stood with the rest of the men on the hill.

"To ancient times, distant music, and prosperous adventures, may we see each other soon," Corbett shouted with tears in his eyes. He could hear the men reply in agreement as he rode toward Ida.

He sniffed back his tears. "Let us go tell the good news to Dem." The three of them set off on a happy trot to Dem's kingdom. Riding away, they turned and waved one last time to their friends. They made great time to Dem's kingdom, arriving late in the evening of the next day.

6

WEDDING BELLS

I da barely contained her excitement as they rode through the forest. Soon she would be married to the most wonderful man she had ever met. They rode over the last of the hills, and there before her stood a magnificent palace. "A palace! I have never seen such a beautiful one or one at all for that matter. Who lives here?" Ida exclaimed excitedly.

"You are not going to believe this, but Dem lives here and is the king of this village. This is the Wooded Kingdom."

At that moment they reached the front steps of the palace, Juliana and Dem were standing there ready to greet them. They had seen the three crest the hill. Juliana was excited that Ida had come, and she looked forward to becoming fast friends with her.

"Ida, you came. It is nice to finally meet you. Please follow me. I will show you where you will be staying until your wedding, which I am sure will be soon, and we will leave these men to do their thing."

Corbett watched until the two chatty women were out of view. It brought a smile to his face and warmness to his heart knowing that Ida would be liked here.

"I see that your decision to have Ida stay behind went well," Dem said with a smile and a playful jab in Corbett's side.

"Yes, I should have known better. Her eyes were too convincing to say no to. There was no way I could go that many days without seeing her. The money you provided us also paid off the remainder of her mother's debt, so we were free to choose what we wanted to do next."

"We hoped that would be enough to sway your decision. It looks like it did," Dem said with a smile.

"Thank you again for that money. We will be planning the wedding for next week. Or I should say she will be planning it. Now that she is with Juliana, they will probably be busy working on that until next week. I can't believe this is all happening. Dem...thank you."

"You are welcome, Corbett. You are my closest friend after all."

The two of them continued talking while they walked to the woodshop.

"You don't have to start the table project yet."

"You should know me enough to know that I can't wait."

"How could I forget? You love this stuff. If you need to take some time and help Ida with whatever she needs, it is fine with me. I am sure Juliana will do the majority of the work—she loves weddings."

The week progressed faster than any week Corbett had ever encountered. William and Hadley joined them a few days after they arrived. Hadley quickly went to work on wedding preparations. Corbett saw Ida for brief moments here and there as their paths crossed. Her wild excitement for the wedding and their new life poured out of her, affecting all around her with a giddy joy. Except for, perhaps, Dem's brother, Irenen, who continued to sulk gloomily around the palace. As the wedding day neared, Corbett's mill friends began to trickle in. They were all there. The day before the wedding, Corbett sat staring out the window in his bedroom. He felt a little nervous about the following day. Would he be the husband Ida needed him to be? Did he have what it takes? He also had silly thoughts of forgetting what to say or tripping over his own feet. He heard his door creak open. He turned around. Dem stood smiling in the doorway.

He sat next to Corbett. "The week has flown by faster than I expected it, which is probably a good thing. Before I forget, I have gifts for you." Dem handed Corbett two smaller boxes.

Corbett opened the boxes. "Wow!" He held in his hand the most ornately carved hunting knife he had ever laid hands on and two beautiful silver-and-diamond wedding bands. "I see that Ida told somebody we had no rings. We were going to buy some, but the week slipped by so fast, we seemed to have run out of time. These are beautiful, and this knife is amazing. Thank you," Corbett said, hugging Dem.

"You are welcome. They were a gift to me from my parents, and I feel they would be just as appreciated by you as they would be by me or my brother. I also have some news for you that I can't wait to share...Juliana is pregnant!" Dem grinned largely.

"Congratulations! What perfect timing. The table will be completed, and we will all be able sit around it exactly as you wished, like one huge family. Again, thank you for the gifts. I can't wait to surprise Ida with the wedding bands. The hunting knife will go nicely with my groomsman outfit. I can't believe I have gone two days without seeing Ida. Tomorrow will be amazing."

"Speaking of tomorrow, I will be joining you in your guest room here. Because tonight..." At this point, all the men from the mill, including William, entered Corbett's living room. "We will be celebrating."

All the men began singing a silly song. The taller men picked Corbett up, placing him above their heads, and they all carried him out of the palace rather loudly.

"Ready to celebrate the night away?" one of the men asked Corbett.

"Umm...I think so." His voice was barely audible over the boisterous group.

Ida watched from her window as the men loudly carried her fiancé away. She smiled, happy that they were all so happy. She, too, had enjoyed a fun evening but much quieter compared to his. Juliana stood by her side. The rest of the ladies had left for the night. Ida had enjoyed a day of pampering with her newfound friends. The evening had come and gone, and as the night stars watched the landscape, she felt tired. With Juliana and Hadley, she continued to watch the boisterous group of men stomp away.

"What a fun sight to see. I am glad though that we had the day we had. I am tired after a day of pampering. How are the two of you feeling?" Hadley said to Juliana and Ida.

"Oh, I feel great but tired. I will probably go to bed soon," Juliana said with a yawn.

"Hope your sleep is restful." Hadley hugged Ida and went to her room.

Juliana and Ida continued to stand and stare into night's dark world. "You sleep well," Juliana said, hugging Ida good night.

"I will. I am so excited for you and Dem. A baby will be so fun. I know we have only known each other a week, but if feels like we have been friends since childhood. I am excited for you, and I am excited for my day tomorrow. Let the adventure begin for the both of us."

"Yes, let it begin. Good night, Ida."

"Good night, Juliana."

Ida crawled into her bed, and for a brief moment, she felt a twinge of foreboding, like the happy moment about to come would not last long. "I must be nervous about tomorrow," she mumbled.

The morning dawned with bright rays and a beaming blue sky. Corbett woke with a start. He could tell the morning was slipping away. He would be getting married today, in just a few hours he guessed. He had wandered into his bed in the wee hours of the morning. The men from the mill lay on all the different pieces of furniture in his room, sleeping. He jumped out of bed to begin his preparations for the wedding ceremony. Dem walked in at that moment, quickly followed by a few male servants carrying brunch.

"Good morning. Hopefully you feel somewhat rested for your big day," Dem said with a knowing grin.

Corbett did not feel hungry, but he did feel rather rested despite arriving to his bed not long ago. He nibbled on a few things. "If you don't mind, let's go get ready now. I don't think I can wait much longer due to my nerves today."

"Then let us all go get ready."

The day began later in the afternoon. By early evening, the entire wedding party was prepared and the ceremony started. Corbett waited at the altar and stood in awe at his beautiful red-haired bride walking down the aisle. The evening sunrays made her hair glisten. Her white dress fit beautifully around her slender curves. Happy tears slipped down both their cheeks as they held each other's hands. The ceremony progressed into the wee hours of the night until the married couple retired to their new home together.

7

SIGHT NOT SEEN

The following days were filled with much joy for everyone in the kingdom. The announcement of the upcoming birth of a royal child combined with the recent wedding sent the village abuzz with excitement. Corbett had taken a few days to celebrate at a secret location provided by Dem, high above the castle on the wooded mountainside. Ida and Corbett gratefully enjoyed the start of their new life together. When they returned, Ida became busy with setting up their new home and helping Juliana with baby preparations. Corbett began his task of building a grand table for the expanding royal family.

The phrase "nine months" kept circling in Corbett's mind as he worked on the table every day. Occasionally, Ida would join him, and they would work side by side.

They loved spending time with each other, although on occasion her fiery personality would clash with his ideas. Nine months seemed like a long time to complete a table, yet not quite long enough as Corbett kept adding new pieces to the soon-to-be grand masterpiece of his woodworking. As he neared completion of the table, which had surprised him by coming sooner than he expected, in the seventh month, he decided to go search for some unique wood, something to set off the oak tree in the center.

As he walked from the palace, he reminisced on his time so far at his new home. At moments, he still could not believe his fortune at having such a friend as Dem. Corbett and Ida still had moments, too, where they felt as if the kingdom had come right out of a storybook. When people entered the kingdom, either by chance or on purpose, they usually remained. With its beauty, the thriving kingdom beckoned people to stay, but the quality of living and the friendly people were a pleasure also.

Corbett's steps had led him to the dark road Dem had warned him about. Corbett paused, staring into the yawning blackness that encompassed the road. A branch snapped. He gazed into the shadows and saw a pair of human eyes that looked strangely familiar staring at him. He blinked, trying to focus, and heard footsteps running away. A glint of something shiny at the edge of the road caught his eye. It looked exactly like what he had been looking for. He stared at the small gold piece of something that looked similar to wood, trying to decide if it was worth ignoring Dem's warnings. Dem had told him this road was where strange, half-mad people entered his kingdom. They were the same people that would trickle into Gilleran every now and then. They passed quickly through the kingdom, ignoring anyone's attempts to assist them, according to Dem.

Corbett just had to have that piece of wood to finish his table masterpiece. Ignoring the cautioning voice of Dem in his head, he stepped forward. Suddenly, an old man came crashing through the forest and stumbled right into Corbett. They collided, causing Corbett to drop the special piece of wood he had just picked up along with everything else he had gathered.

"Wow, are you hurt?" Corbett stood and reached down to help the ragged and thin old man.

The man turned and looked at Corbett with a cold, empty stare that pierced Corbett's mind. The instant Corbett touched him, an image flashed through his mind, much like the day when he touched that strange sword so long ago. He saw King Dem in a field on his knees, yelling. Then his mind flashed to images of Juliana's portraits covered in cobwebs. Images flitted and flashed across his mind. A cradle in Juliana's room sat empty and covered with dust. Then Irenen's face with a huge grin filled Corbett's mind until he let out an audible yell and let go of the strange man's hand. He looked directly at the old man, trying to see any familiarity with the man he had encountered so many years ago coming into Gilleran.

The ragged old man burst out, "Ah...what have you done? I see, I see, I see. They come. Who comes? From the depth and the dark, they seek and thirst. I see, I see."

He hobbled on his weak legs and spoke nonsense at Corbett.

Corbett swayed on his feet a moment after releasing the ragged old man's hand and took a moment to gather his fractured thoughts. "No, wait. What have you done? I saw something, too. What is coming?" Corbett asked as the man danced on his wobbly legs in front of him. The man cackled an ancient laugh in response.

"No, what have you done? I saw something, too. They come for him. Ha-ha." The old man danced around Corbett and started to walk away. His face haunting as he taunted Corbett.

"Wait, I can help you." Corbett reached out his hand to take hold of the old man, but another image flashed in his mind. This time Irenen held a hand over his heart. By the time Corbett gathered his wits about him, the old man had danced his odd dance into the forest. Corbett could hear him singing.

"I see, I see, from the depth and the dark. They seek and thirst. Cold and dark he who is brother..." The last bit of the song whispered through the forest and could not be heard.

Corbett shouted, "He who is brother to whom...to what?"

The only response was a faint "I see, I see."

Corbett felt cold and drained. He barely had enough energy to pick up his little piece of wood along with the other small sticks he had gathered. He routinely walked toward the palace and was greeted by a few of the castle guards.

"Corbett? Are you OK? Here, let me get that for you," one on the guards said after seeing Corbett's pale face and blank stare.

It took Corbett a moment to answer and realize he did not have the wood in his arms any longer. "You know those stories Dem tells of the dark road and the half-mad people? I just encountered one of them. Do they usually speak to people?" Corbett whispered shakily.

"No. If they say anything, it never makes any sense. Why? Did this person say something to you?" asked the guard.

"Yes, and I'm not sure if it makes sense. It gave me a cold feeling throughout my body. The gravelly old man's voice is stuck in my head, and his cold empty eyes. I don't know. It gives me a foreboding feeling."

"Let us find Dem while you wait in the dining room." The guards put the wood in the dining room by the table and left Corbett sitting on his work stool. Corbett sat perfectly still in the quiet dining hall, the eerie song filling his mind. He tried to focus on finishing one of the roses on the table but could not think of anything but the haunting song in his head. He should have heeded Dem's caution about the dark road, but this little piece of wood was perfect for his table. He looked down in his hand at the pretty gold piece of wood. He smiled, thinking it was still worth it. He stood and turned as Dem and the guards walked into the room, glad to have his mind focused on something else.

"Corbett, please tell me what happened. Usually people that enter my kingdom by that dark road say little. They are usually so crazy they refuse help and proceed into the forest unharmed to wander as they wish." Dem spoke directly to the pale and shaky Corbett.

"I think once I tell you my tale, I will take a day off with Ida to rest." Corbett could wait no longer, and events of his day tumbled out of his mouth. "This ragged old man ran into me, running from something. I reached down to help him since we collided with each other, and every time I touched his arm, I saw images. I saw you kneeling in a field in sadness, cobwebs on Juliana's portraits, an empty cradle and your brother's grinning face."

"Interesting. What happened next?" Dem said while slowly pacing the room.

"Then the old man sang to me and danced around me. The song is stuck in my head. 'Ah...what have you done. I see, I see, I see. They come. Who comes? From the depth and the dark, they seek and thirst. I see, I see.' Then I tried to ask him what he did to me and who comes for whom, and he repeated whatever I said back. Singing 'No, what have you done? I saw something, too. They come for him. Ha-ha.' The last part of the song I heard floating in the air as he danced back into the forest was, 'I see, I see. From the depth and the dark, they seek and thirst. Cold and dark he who is brother...' I yelled, 'He is brother to whom or what?' and the reply that came faintly in the air was, 'I see, I see.'"

"Is that it? Did you get a name from him?"

"That is everything, no name. I apologize for not heeding your caution about the dark road. That rose will sure be extra special on your table though." Corbett pointed at the table but continued staring down at his feet.

Dem listened, pacing the floor in deep thought, occasionally rubbing his chin. "Guards, go see if you can locate my brother. I am thinking he might know something about this. It is no secret that he and I are not as close as we once were, but I would like to hear his take on this strange encounter. I have not seen him in a while, so he may be hard to locate."

"Oh, I think I did see someone watching me before this strange man appeared. But he ran away before I could be sure. Do you think it could have been Irenen?"

"Perhaps. Corbett, you are more than welcome to have the rest you asked for. Take a few extra days if you need to. You do not have to worry about the table if you need a little time to gather yourself—"

"I want to work on the table. I will not have my seven-month project looking anything less than perfect for the week's big reveal!" The emotions from his day overcame him, getting the better of him in his overly dramatic reply to Dem.

"Don't worry. I was not commanding you to rest, just acknowledging your request. If you feel up to working, that is fine with me. About what happened when you touched the old man, that is a gift that only a few of the members of my kingdom have. Has that happened before?"

"Yes but a very long time ago."

"That is very interesting that you have the gift since you are not originally from here. We will have to discuss that more a little later. I would like to focus on finding my brother at the moment, and I need to make a visit to the library. Would you like to go see Ida or join me in the library?"

"If you don't mind, Dem, I would enjoy seeing my wife and then finishing the table. Maybe tomorrow. Maybe rest will clear my mind of this strange song."

"I don't mind. I will let you know if I find anything if I see you before dinner, and maybe we can discuss it tomorrow. I am sure the table will look amazing; I can't imagine what else you need to do to such a large and lovely table. I am sure I will be surprised."

"You will be. Good luck on your search for answers."

"Thanks." Dem patted Corbett on the shoulder as he exited the dining room.

Corbett retired to his bed but not before sharing his strange encounter with Ida.

"Let's go out there right now and search for that man. Nobody should ever talk to you that way." Ida stepped out of the bed passionately, ready to track down the strange man.

"No, now is not the time, come sleep with me. My day has worn me out."

With a huff, Ida lay back down, the snuggles from Corbett calming her, and they slowly drifted to sleep.

When the first rays of sun peeked through Corbett's windows, he awoke with a start. He had continued dreaming of his strange encounter, even though it had occurred a few days ago. Today he felt more rested than he had. He kissed Ida good morning, got ready, and went into the dining room. Today would be the big reveal.

He stood in the large dining hall, and he shook himself a little to get himself to start thinking about the
table and focusing on his last task. He pulled out a large
burlap bag that he had hiding under his workbench
and opened it. He gazed upon hundreds of intricately
carved dark wooden roses and rose petals that Ida had
also helped him with. He had counted them early the
day before and needed one more rose petal to complete
the effect he wanted to create on the center of the table.

Corbett walked over to the large wooden table and
pulled off all the different cloths he had used to hide
it. He had worked hard at keeping the final project a
secret from not only the king but all the other members
of the castle. The staff knew that today they were not
allowed in the dining hall at all until the absolute last
minute that would allow them enough time to decorate
the room. The big reveal party would be soon if all went
according to Corbett's plans. It felt good to be so close to
finishing and early no less. Only two more months until
the royal baby would be born.

After pulling off all eighteen tablecloths, Corbett
sighed and gazed at his masterpiece. The dark wooden
table gleamed under the grand lights. Raised tree carvings wrapped around the legs and swooped along the
edges. Then Corbett's eyes rested on the center, where a
large oak tree was carved, which would have rose petals
falling from its branches appearing to cascade onto the
floor. Corbett hoped Dem would like the roses more than
leaves. Somehow the roses seemed to bring together the
feel of elegance and create an air of mystery, which he
felt would be fitting for this place. Corbett began the

task of adding the small carved roses around the edges of the table; he would glue the rosebuds to the legs of the table to give an appearance of blossoming flowers and would end with the large oak tree. He had a lot of work to do before dinner but knew he could do it, making sure to leave enough time to carve the only leaf that would adorn the oak tree in the unusual piece of wood he had found. His excitement about revealing his masterpiece was combined with a little nervousness. What if Dem did not like it, or Juliana, or both of them? He pushed that nonproductive thought aside.

"Here we go," he said as he attached more roses to the table. His mind became focused on his project.

8

SEARCHING

After Dem told Juliana about Corbett's strange encounter, he remembered the book his father used to read to him and Irenen when they were young boys. He loved listening to the stories his father read out of that book. Fond memories washed over him as he remembered sitting with Irenen, listening to the deep, soothing sound of his father's voice speak of the truth that hid away in stories. He put the book in the library years ago after his father passed away. It seemed the right place to store it for others to enjoy.

As he walked down the hallway after sleeping restfully, he thought there might be an old prophecy in the book that talked about a strange song or a strange man that he could not quite remember. His mind wandered with different thoughts. It had been a long time since he had read that book. His mind began to mull over the images Corbett had seen. The one that most disturbed him was the smiling face of Irenen. Irenen had become distant since Juliana's pregnancy. Dem knew Irenen desired the throne, but he would not inherit it since Dem would soon have an heir. As children, Irenen and Dem got along, but as their father continued to read that book through their childhood, Irenen would dwell more on the details of power and less on the overall story of how the kingdom came to be. As they got older, Irenen had become unsatisfied at their father's lack of desire to change the rules of the kingdom that had helped make it such a success in the first place. The sudden death of their father had brought wisdom to Dem he felt, but to Irenen, it had brought an increased desire for power and a small inkling of something dark brewing inside him.

One time, Dem had wondered if Irenen had something to do with their father's death. He had been healthy for a man over three hundred years old, and one day, he seemingly died in his sleep. Dem knew he had been ready to pass but always had a nagging feeling that he could have lived a lot longer and one day shared in the joy of meeting his grandson or granddaughter. It was rare for their genealogy to have somebody die before their five hundredth birthday. The royal line came from an ancient race that was all but extinct due to a mysterious sickness. Dem still remembered the day his mother died shortly after giving birth to his brother. She had only been two hundred. Dem was about ten when Irenen was born, and he smiled, remembering how excited he had been to become a big brother. The month that Irenen was born, his mother became ill. She had been unable to sleep early in the pregnancy due to nightmares that she would share with no one, not even his father.

Dem still remembers his father coming to get him one cold early January morning.

A violent snowstorm howled outside, and the castle windows shook as they were coated with ice. His father picked him up and walked him briskly to his mother's room. "Demeerco, you are a big brother. We will go meet your baby brother, but your mother is ill. Make sure you tell her you love her."

He could still remember being set down by his father and walking into his mother's room. Attendants stood around her, fussing over her, and he could see the sickly pale color in her skin. But her eyes still lit up when he entered the room.

"My lovely Demeerco, come meet your little brother," she whispered weakly.

"What is his name, Mother?" he whispered back.

"Irenen. Prince Irenen. Do you like him?" she whispered again.

"Yes. I will be the best big brother ever. I love you, Mother, and I will take good care of him." He knew at that young age that his mother was sickly, and he wanted to comfort her.

She leaned over and hugged and kissed him, letting warm tears splash across his face. "I love you, too, sweetest Demmy. Be a good little prince for your father."

"I will, Mother." He hugged her one more time and grabbed little Irenen's small hand. Irenen opened his eyes, and they were the darkest eyes Dem could remember ever seeing. Then he was ushered away, back to his room.

His father did well raising his brother from birth and Dem from the age of ten. Dem grew up fast and helped wherever and however he'd been needed. His parents had always desired another child to preserve the bloodline as long as possible. Not many of his family members ever had more than one child. So when Dem's father had sons, the kingdom's people were elated. The passing of his mother had been hard for everyone, but they all recovered quickly to take care of little Prince Irenen. He was a fussy baby and prone to sickness. Dem and Irenen had a happy childhood in spite of a sad beginning. But as Irenen became older, he secluded himself to wandering in the forest late at night, and then when he would return, he would be distant.

Dem arrived at the library door, still pondering his past when he noticed his pregnant wife sitting in a reading chair. A smile spread across his face.

Sun streamed through the windows that revealed a magnificent waterfall. The windows were open, and a breeze lightly blew the curtain. The smell of fresh air filled the room. Juliana sat on a red velvet chair near the open window, reading a book quietly.

"Hi, my love." Dem leaned down and kissed the top of her head. "What brings you to the library on such a beautiful day?" Dem asked.

"I decided to read a story to our child while I rested my feet. It must be making this little one inside me excited; he keeps jumping. I can't wait until we get to meet this busy little one." Juliana rubbed her stomach gently.

"I can't wait my beautiful wife. Do you think the little one will be a son or a daughter?" Dem gently rubbed Juliana's belly.

"I think either way I will be happy. But my excitement grows every day. I feel like the little one will be a boy, but we won't know until the eventful day finally arrives. What brings you to the library, my sweet husband?"

"I am looking for the storybook my father used to read to me as a child. The encounter Corbett had with that strange man in the woods reminded me of that story. I am not sure if I will find what I am looking for in its pages, but I wanted to double-check. Plus it will be a good story to read to our little one soon."

"That's interesting because I have been reading that book to our child. It seemed appropriate since that is what your father did with you. But today when I came in here, the spot where it goes was empty. I asked around to see if someone had mistakenly removed it from the library, but no one had. So today I settled for a simple children's story."

"I will take a look around and see if perhaps someone has misplaced it." Dem muttered under his breath his annoyance with the book being misplaced after an hour of searching the dusty shelves, "The books are rarely allowed to leave the library. Who would remove it?"

"What was that Dem? You are mumbling? Did you find the book?"

"No. The book is not here. I am sorry for disturbing you, my dear."

"I don't mind. I hope you find it. I do love that book. We should keep a copy in our private room. I wonder whatever happened to Irenen's copy."

"That's right; I forgot Irenen had a copy. I will keep looking on the shelf for my copy. Enjoy your reading time, the both of you." Dem smiled as he leaned in and kissed Juliana, patting her stomach.

"We will." Juliana kissed Dem before he continued about his day.

Dem walked to the history section of the library, and one of the guards entered the room. "We were unable to locate Irenen, sir. We have searched throughout the castle, and he is nowhere to be found."

The book, too, was missing and nowhere to be found on any of the shelves. Interesting, Dem thought.

Juliana came behind Dem and rubbed his back. "Did the guards find the book, honey?"

"No, they did not find the book or Irenen either. Hopefully I can ask Irenen about it before tonight. What are you doing the rest of the day?"

"I think I might go figure out what to wear for our fun evening and then get ready. I can't wait to see the table. I bet it will be absolutely amazing." Juliana grabbed Dem's hand and began walking toward the library door. "Come spend the rest of the day with me."

Dem thought about continuing his search for the book, but he couldn't resist his cute, pregnant wife. "I think that sounds like a fine idea," Dem said as they walked hand in hand to their room.

The evening progressed quickly and the time for the big reveal had finally come. Dem excitedly anticipated the evening festivities with Juliana. He allowed his mind to shift, thinking of the more serious matters at hand for a brief moment. *Hopefully, Irenen will be at the dinner tonight. I can speak with him then*, he thought, as he had yet to track down the book or Irenen, both of which he found disconcerting.

9

DARKNESS TAKES HOLD

Irenen sat on a rock, staring at the large white palace that belonged to him. He did not want to attend the dinner his brother had invited him to. He felt angry and bitter that his brother would have an heir that would inherit the throne. Irenen's thoughts were filled with how he should be the one on the throne. He had the desire for the power the kingdom needed to be unrivaled by any other in the land. He knew that his desire for power would increase their already plentiful resources and secure their position with the surrounding kingdoms, even acquiring some of their lands. Maybe it would restore their once great lineage. A small smirk spread across his face as he remembered the last argument he had with his father about power so many years ago. Then a delightful shiver crept through his body.

"I think perhaps...I will go to the dinner tonight," he said, deep in thought. Irenen grabbed a small bag he had with him and took it to his secret hideout. Near the boulder he had been sitting upon, years ago he had carved a hideout underground so he could have something to call his own. He didn't want to have to share everything. He opened the secret door, lit a small lantern, and climbed down the narrowly carved dirt stairs. He took a deep breath, and the smell of cold, damp earth filled his nose. He loved that smell. Here were all his things: jars of old mushrooms, containers of poisonous snakes, and a few maps he had made of the dark roads. Dark roads no one else dared to travel upon. In his lonely walks, he had discovered an ancient realm he hoped the Wooded Kingdom would soon embrace.

He had been around the corner when Corbett told Dem what had transpired in the woods when he had gone searching for some wood; it inspired a spiteful idea. He would add his latest item. He reached into his bag and pulled out a book he had taken from the library. Opening the front cover, he read, "To Prince Dem. Remember, always, the place your ancestors created and how you came to be. Love, your father." Irenen loved taking Dem's things. "Ha," he said as he set the book on a shelf next to his, smiling as the two volumes graced his dusty shelves. The dinner bell rang loudly outside of the castle and faintly interrupted his dark thoughts. Irenen looked down at his clothes. They were somewhat disheveled but would pass for the dinner party. Besides, he was a prince and could do as he wished. He climbed the narrow stairs, closed the secret door again, and hid his extinguished lantern. Then he brushed himself off and started walking to the dinner party.

Corbett stood next to the gleaming dinner table with Ida by his side. The wood shined in the lights around the dining room. Plate settings would be set for 122 people in total. The table had become larger than he had anticipated, but it looked beautiful.

"What do you think?" Corbett squeezed her hand as they both gazed at the table.

"Hmmm...let's see it is a little off center, no I'm joking dear. It is amazing! I am glad the timing worked out for me to see it before I leave to go help my mother move. Don't you for one second feel bad about not coming with me. I will leave early tomorrow morning and hope to be back in a month's time. I love you, my dear, more than you know. Let's celebrate your amazing accomplishment." Ida gave him a forceful kiss on the lips.

Corbett smoothed out his clothes one last time as the attendants opened the dining room doors. King Dem and Juliana were the first to walk through. The table's smooth finish caught their eyes. As they got closer, they noticed that the intricate details of the roses and trees were amazing. They slowly walked around the table and stopped, mesmerized at the magnificent oak tree carved in the center. The tree leaves were cascading rose petals, and one gold leaf glinted and gleamed.

Juliana walked over to Corbett and gave him a huge hug. "This is simply amazing. Almost magical in the way it appears. Thank you."

Dem also walked over to him and gave him a big hug. "You didn't tell me you were a magician, my friend. This is more than we could have ever asked for. Thank you!" Dem said as he ran his hand over a few of the rosebuds. He turned to one of the attendants and said, "Open the doors, and let the guests in. Let's have some dinner!"

As the doors opened, the guests started pouring in. Corbett, Ida, Dem, and Juliana sat at the head of the table and watched with excitement as the guests came in. One chair remained empty next to Dem. It seemed as if the entire village stood in the large dining room. Corbett felt honored by the reactions people had at the sight of the table. Other tables had been brought in for the overflow of people, which flowed out the doors. When all the guests were almost seated, Irenen came slinking in. Dem and Juliana were busy in conversation, but Corbett noticed Irenen. His demeanor seemed cold, and the way his unnaturally dark eyes scanned the room and stopped on Juliana made Corbett squirm inside. He wished he could pinpoint the exact reason Irenen invoked this response. Irenen heavily plopped down on his seat next to Dem.

Dem sensed his brother's presence. "Irenen, thank you for coming tonight. I was wondering if you know—"

"Dinner is served," announced one of the attendants.

"I'll ask you after dinner," Dem said quickly.

Dinner proceeded with one course after the next, and the amount of enthusiasm in the room grew with each new platter. Corbett was amazed that the food didn't seem to run out. There had been a lengthy break in between the appetizer course and the main course to allow for more visiting. Many guests thanked Dem and Juliana for the invitation to the dinner. It also allowed time for Corbett to answer the many, if not the same, questions from the guests: "How long did the table take to complete?" "Where did you get the idea?" "What type of wood is it made out of?" But he was happy to answer any questions the villagers had. A bell rang to prompt everyone to sit down as the main course was brought out.

As the joy gleefully flitted unseen through the air, there was one who did not find the current events joyful. Irenen had gloomily attended the wedding of Dem's new friends. He had listened reluctantly to the announcement of the upcoming royal birth and now he felt forgotten in the hustle and bustle of the joy-filled room. He had attended the special dinner out of obligation to the kingdom, not his brother. As Irenen watched Dem laughing with Corbett and hugging Juliana, he couldn't stand it anymore and left. An encounter with Corbett had helped make his final decision to leave.

Dem leaned over and whispered to Corbett, "Does my brother seem uncharacteristically unhappy tonight?"

"It is hard to say with your brother. I don't know him well, but he does seem bothered by something."

"Hmm...I never know what is wrong with him. Interesting that he hasn't filled his seat yet. Did you see him leave?" Dem inquired as the first plates of roast duck and succulent pig were carried out.

"I did see him get up quickly when we were dismissed for a few minutes. I had been watching him because he seemed to leave in such a hurry that I thought he had gotten ill. Maybe he went to his room." What Corbett didn't tell Dem was that when he greeted Irenen and shook his hand, he had another picture flash in his mind, much like the one when he encountered the strange man in the woods. It was a flash of Irenen smiling and his head bent back in a rapturous laugh while he was surrounded by darkness. Then an image of an old man lying on the floor with Irenen smiling down on him appeared. The image blurred, like looking through a morning mist, and a ruined castle flashed in his mind, and then he was standing holding Irenen's hand awkwardly.

Irenen had not said a word during or after the encounter, but he lingered in front of Corbett with a look of anger that sent a chill coursing through Corbett's body. Then Irenen spoke, "I saw—"

At that moment, a guest had come up to Corbett to congratulate him on the table. By the time Corbett turned to go to his seat, Irenen had already seated himself and stared heavily in Corbett's direction. That is why Corbett had kept an eye on Irenen during dinner. He would tell Dem but not now. This was a special night. In the morning, he would share what had transpired.

"I will have one of the attendants go check his room to make sure he is well. This is strange behavior for Irenen. He usually never passes up a chance to eat."

More duck and steamed sweet potatoes were added to the already full plates. It was a feast to be remembered.

Irenen knew that Corbett saw the same images that had flashed in his own mind as they shook hands. He had seen them once before, the morning of his father's death when his father had given him an out-of-the-ordinary hug and thanked him for being his son. It had shocked Irenen because his father hardly ever behaved in that matter. He remembered how it had given him the courage to approach him later in the day with one of his ideas. An idea that had ended in a heated argument the first time he presented it to him years ago. A second time, that evening, he presented his ideas of conducting experiments to gain more power by using the ways that were outlawed long ago. He replayed the conversation in his mind like he had done many times since that day.

"Father, don't you see our ancestors were onto something. The books I found in those old ruins spoke of harnessing a creature's power that would make the kingdom stronger than any other. They only needed willing subjects to participate in the procedure."

His father shook his head, anger flashing in his eyes. "And what happens when the willing subjects run out! Son, those ways were not lost to us. They were forgotten for a reason. That ancient realm is ours, true, but it represents a dark spot on our history. Why do you think there are so few of us now? Those creatures they used consumed their minds with warped ways of thinking, the experiments crossed lines that should have never been crossed. That land is in ruins for a reason." The king reached out a hand and rested it on Irenen's shoulder, earnestly seeking for understanding in those dark eyes that he never understood. "You are forbidden to return there." He stepped away, turning his back to Irenen.

"But, Father, don't you see that ancient realm, the knowledge in those books, I could conduct the experiments once again but in relative seclusion. I could find another way if subjects weren't willing."

"How could any son of mine desire such a dark way of obtaining power?" he had whispered, staring into Irenen's eyes. Irenen remembered the confidence he felt and the certainty that his father would like his idea after that conversation. But when his father replied with disgust, it broke an invisible wall inside him that he had long fought against. That moment hurt more than Irenen had ever shared except within the dark corners of his secret hideout. The anger coursed through his veins, and he smiled as he saw his father lying on the ground. To this day, nobody knew the truth of what truly happened to the king. He would prove to his dead father that he could create the most powerful kingdom anyone has ever seen, that the old ways had existed for a purpose.

He decided he would follow through with the idea he had presented to his father so many years ago. One key change would set this idea apart. He would not join with the Wooded Kingdom. He would start a new kingdom, and this kingdom would swallow his brother's. This would be his own great kingdom, and he knew exactly where he would go. He would walk the dark road to the ruins he had discovered. That would be his home from now on. Irenen knew what Corbett had seen earlier because he too had touched the old man that day. He had seen the power that he could have and would take it. Corbett, or anyone else for that matter, wouldn't be able to stop him. He opened the palace doors, walked out, and never looked back.

10

LIVES COLLIDE

Corbett closed his eyes and thought of happier times so long ago. What had it been—eighteen years since he had seen his beautiful passionate Ida? Sitting in his quaint cabin, Corbett's eyes focused on tending the fire in the hearth. A fire seemed in order for a little added comfort to this cold night.

Corbett sighed. Morning had come to his little cabin while he had been lost in thought. He must have finally dozed off at some point when the stars were high in the evening sky. Corbett stood and stretched a nice long stretch. His cabin still felt cold. He walked to his front door and opened it. It was day, but the sun hid behind a late spring of snow-filled clouds. He looked to the distance and could see the old castle bathed in beautiful sunlight. Winter never touched that area. His breath became little white puffs in the air as he hurriedly grabbed more wood for the fire. He wondered how long this cold would last on this side of the great rip in the earth. The weather here had always been fickle, but the cold seemed to linger the longest. Corbett resided in the one home that had escaped the long-ago war. It could be sunny one minute with birds signing, and then, within the same day, there could be a blizzard, almost as if the land had been enchanted. The extreme weather gave him the seclusion he had desired for so many years. Soon, though, he would walk in the land again in confidence, ending the days of his hiding, allowing him to go search for his long-lost friends.

He got up from tending the fire, pulled his wooden chair nearer, and propped his socked feet near the hearth. Corbett closed his eyes and started to let the day's chill thaw from his limbs. As he rested, he began to think about his life. He smiled as he remembered meeting William for the first time and becoming accustomed to work at the mill. His mind floated to his wife, Ida. They adored each other. A small but sad smile crept across his lips. He had robbed her of so many years they could have spent together. Then his memory flitted back to his closest friend, Dem, and he made himself chuckle as he remembered his first interaction with him. He missed him but still knew, so many years later, that he had made the right decision to leave. He opened his eyes, tended to the fire again, and reclined back in his chair, lost in thought.

Corbett startled awake. He wondered how long he had been lost in sleeping thought. His fire had died down to a few glowing embers. He got out of his wooden chair and opened his front door. It was dark out, and the full moon glistened on the small pond in front of his cabin. Another day had passed quickly. Corbett took a few deep breaths of the crisp night air. He had slept the entire day away, but considering the eventful day before, when he'd rescued his guest, he knew why he needed the sleep. He grabbed a few more logs, carried them into the house, and laid them by the fire. As he stretched, his gaze stopped at his bed. His guest still slept comfortably in it. Before making himself something to eat, he checked on his guest again. She was still cold, but the color had crept back into her skin. He put another blanket on her. Tears formed in his eyes as he stared at her.

Wiping away a few tears, he focused and started the fire to clear the chill. As he ate, his mind began to meander in thought, lingering on his short time in the Wooded Kingdom. It seemed such a distant memory that it felt more like a dream. He could hear his guest stirring, but he stared into the fire, focused on his food.

The smell of a freshly lit fire floated through the air and awakened the thawing senses of Corbett's guest. She slowly opened her blurry eyes and was greeted by a rustic cabin. She must have been dreaming because the man at the fire looked like the back of her husband. Her husband had been dead for years, or wait...maybe his death had been a dream. She opened her parched mouth and spoke to the man in her dream. "Hello..." She tried to roll over to get a better look at him.

Corbett stood quickly and walked to the side of the bed. "Shh...lie still. Here, try to sip some of this warm water."

She obeyed, and the warm water felt soothing on her insides. As she tentatively reached her hand out, she touched the man's whiskery face. His blue eyes looked intently at her.

"Corbett? Is this really you, or am I dreaming?"

Corbett stayed silent for a moment. He gently helped her lie back in the bed. "Yes, Ida, it is me, Corbett, and no, this is not a dream. Rest. There will be time for questions later."

As she lay back down, Ida whispered, "I remember walking in the snow, and a fire, and then everything went black. Rest? I must be dreaming; this is not possible." Ida closed her eyes and went back to sleep quickly.

Corbett watched her fall asleep. He felt as if this were a dream, too. He felt horrible for what Ida had come to believe, but he had no control of what happened at the beginning of his plans so long ago. He remembered as he stared into the fire once more.

After seeing the images that day he shook Irenen's hand combined with the strange encounters with the man in the woods, it had helped him to see Irenen's quest for power. He had planned on telling Dem at once and perhaps searching the kingdom's surrounding land for him. But as time would have it, the royal birth came sooner than expected with Juliana being pregnant with twins, much to the disappointment of Ida, who had been at her mother's at the time, so he awaited his time to tell Dem when it was more appropriate. He had hoped to tell Dem after the royal baby shower, but Irenen arrived unexpectedly and stole the children. He tried to stop the kidnapping of the royal children but had been caught by one of Irenen's dreadful men before he could give chase. Those men took the boots right off his feet. They came at him from all sides. One carried a burlap bag. He was knocked to the ground, and as he lay there struggling, he saw his beloved mill being set on fire and the men strategically placing his boots in a location where he knew others would think he had died. Then it all went dark for a long time.

He had been thankful that no one had come searching for him, worried about what Irenen would do if anyone should venture into that dark realm...Days and nights passed. Corbett couldn't tell how long he had been in Irenen's dungeon, but a day came when he found a way to escape and took it. He knew the way to Dem's kingdom was being watched by Irenen's men, so that day Corbett stumbled along a barely visible, old path on a long trek through an unfamiliar land, finally finding the house he resided in.

It took him many days to recover from what Irenen had done to him. Corbett felt lucky he had been able to escape before Irenen had succeeded in whatever he was experimenting with. As he took time and recovered, he explored and found an ancient road that eventually led him another way to the Wooded Kingdom. He remembered standing behind some trees, gazing at his once beautiful home. He wandered around unnoticed, hoping to find Ida, but she was gone. His beloved workshop was gone, and the kingdom seemed empty, older, too. He wanted to remain unknown in case Irenen came searching for him and attacked this place once again.

He inquired around about Ida. He only questioned a few villagers so he would not raise suspicion. He discovered she remained with her mother after the presumed death of Corbett. He quickly rode to William's that day in hopes of finding Ida there. Tears slipped from his closed eyes as he remembered the scene that greeted him, the scene that still flashed in his nightmares. The mill lay in shambles across from him. Nothing existed of his home, and William's house had been completely burnt down. He did not realize how long he had been gone.

"Irenen!" he screamed that day, and then began his search once again for answers in the town of Gilleran.

In Gilleran, he stopped at the other mill and found a few of his fellow mill workers. They greeted him with happy tears in their eyes and recounted a sad tale of how a strange man with frightening large creatures burst out of the woods on a late afternoon, setting ablaze all that stood in their way, focusing their anger on the mill. They all fought hard to save the mill, but in the end, the fire consumed everything, including some of the mill workers and William and Hadley. The ache that formed in Corbett's heart that day lingered with him always, but he welcomed it as a reminder of loved ones and happier moments.

Corbett brought his chair over from the fire and sat next to Ida's bed, keeping a watchful eye on her, noting that her beautiful head of red hair had a few white strands running through it. More color had crept into her face. Corbett felt some of the tension in his shoulders relax as he noticed Ida looking a little better. He did not want to leave her side and stared out the frosted window as he sat beside the bed.

Ida opened her eyes again. She could feel warmth in her body. She gingerly tried to sit up.

"Here, let me help you. You are still quite weak from your ordeal."

"How long have I been asleep?"

"About two days. Are you hungry?"

"Yes, but I need some water. Would you feel like telling me where you have been for so many years? I have missed you greatly. I am not angry. I have a feeling Irenen had something to do with this. If he did, we will find him," she said with sharpness on her tongue.

Corbett gave her a glass of water and set a bowl of soup near her. "I will begin at the end since that will make more sense. I am in this cabin today because I ran from captivity at Irenen's ruthless hand. He captured..."

Corbett's story weaved in the cabin's air. Ida joined her story with his at times. They both shared their lives into the wee hours of the night, still feeling as if this was a dream.

"Ida, I did search for you, but I did not realize I had been in Irenen's captivity for so many years. I went everywhere I thought you would be, and you were nowhere to be found. I did not want to draw too much attention because I knew Irenen would destroy anyone I found."

"That was very wise."

"I am so sorry I remained hidden for as long as I did. It was by chance three days ago that I encountered a strange man in the woods who spoke in nonsensical riddles, but he did say a town's name throughout his riddle. I am glad I followed the name to the town, which I came upon in a horrible snowstorm. I could see a flaming house in the distance. I knew without a doubt you were there. I rushed through the storm, only barely releasing you from your chains before the house collapsed. How the chains became undone is still a mystery to me. Somebody was watching out for us."

"Thank you for saving me. If I had known you were still alive, I would have searched for you. All those years Irenen robbed us of. He needs to answer for what he has done."

"He will someday but not today. Please continue."

"I was heartbroken the day I received word of your death. The announcement of the birth reached me, but it said nothing of twins. I felt so guilty for having been with my mother when everything bad transpired in the Wooded Kingdom that I just stayed away, telling myself that one day I would return. To be honest, I became a shell of my former self, my passion for life hiding for a long time." Corbett reached over and rested his hand on Ida's leg. "Then time continued to move on, and I said one day I would return less and less until you and our happy life were but a distant memory. Then one day as I walked in the forest, I discovered something very strange in a clearing—twin babies. Not knowing they belonged to Dem and Juliana, I felt they were safer with me at my home with my mother."

"So how did you end up in the house I found you at?"

"Then, a little while after finding the twins, I relocated again to a neighboring town to start over after my mother's death and continued to raise the twins as my own. They gave me something to live for once again. Then that detestable solider came, and he would have destroyed all of us if he had his way. Thank you again for saving me. The twins, I hope they are safe." She looked around the room sadly and quietly whispered, "I sent them into the woods."

11

AKEYERA

Akeyera closed her eyes as her horse lightly plodded on the cold, hard ground, trying to picture the kingdom she was taken from so long ago. Images of a faded gray castle and a tumbling forest came to her mind, but that was all. Her memory of that life had all but disappeared. She opened her eyes and gazed at the land before her. Spring peeked through patches of melting snow on the path. Happy green sprigs of grass, the small spots of color, brought warmness to her heart.

She held up her hand, causing the line of troops behind her to halt. They were standing near a wide but shallow stream. "Let us take lunch here. We have about a day left from this point, I think." The last part of her sentence was barely audible.

They had been traveling through the land for a few weeks, afraid to stop for prolonged periods due to the constant sightings of Irenen's men. They had not been sighted for about a week, however, so Akeyera hoped they had given up their relentless chase. A memory stirred in her mind at the sight of the two large boulders on the other side of the stream, of a small, giggly girl saying to a tall man with a crown on his brow, *Daddy, Daddy, we are almost home. Mother will be so happy with the beautiful deer we will bring for dinner tonight.*

Yes, sweetie. One more night in the wood and tomorrow we will be home...

The memory faded. Akeyera wanted so badly to tell the many people around her, but she knew it would only cause doubt to enter everyone's minds. She had not told anyone of her doubts on which way they were going or if her kingdom still existed. She kept relying on distant memories and faded dreams for direction, and so far it had been working. This latest memory of life so long ago brought tears to her eyes. She wondered what had happened in the time she had been away. She shook her head to stop thinking the worst.

"Akeyera, this land looks like it is waking from winter's hold. It is refreshing to see the colors of spring again, even if it is only a few sprigs of grass here and there," Conall said.

"Yes, I agree. It has been nice to find fresh water with plenty of fish for our travels, too. Without it, our supplies would have diminished long ago. We will be in my kingdom by nightfall tomorrow," Akeyera said with a note of hesitation in her voice.

"What do you think your kingdom will be like after you've been gone for so long?" Conall asked quizzically.

Akeyera looked around her. Conall was the only one near. She needed to confide in someone, anyone, before she just burst out everything she was keeping inside. She lowered her voice to a whisper and leaned toward Conall. "Honestly I am unsure of what to expect, but I am hopeful for a warm greeting. It has been many years since I have dwelt there, and I cannot guarantee that we will be greeted warmly or that anyone is left."

Conall was shocked at her candidness. She pretty much kept to herself; if she wasn't discussing the next move, she was silent. "Whatever the state of your kingdom, I know I am happy with you leading us there."

"Please do not tell the others of my doubts. I know, somehow, this is the way, but that's about all I know at this point."

"Don't worry, I will honor your request. The farther Irenen's kingdom is from us the better. Hopefully we can recuperate quickly and come up with another plan to go rescue my sister." Conall leaned in and whispered, "Again, I will not share your concerns. Anytime you need to talk about anything, I am here for you. I am sure the others would also understand. We are all in this together."

Akeyera breathed a sigh of relief over Conall's response. "Yes, a time to recuperate will be good for all of us."

"I also want you to know that if your kingdom is not what you expected, I am still happy you had a place to take us to," Conall said in between bites of steamed fish.

"We all are happy to put that foul place behind us," said a soldier walking toward them with a group of soldiers. The soldiers joined them and sat to eat their meals.

"I am glad. I needed to hear that. I better go grab some of that fish before it is gone."

Akeyera walked over to Derek, who was serving the meals. "You never cease to amaze me, Derek. We have only been stopped for a few minutes, and already you have this amazing concoction of fish and herbs whipped into a delicious meal," Akeyera said while blowing gingerly on the steaming bowl of food.

"It is a learned talent from working for the kingdom for so many years. Thank you." Derek surveyed the crowd, making sure everyone had food, and grabbed that last bowl for himself. He sat next to his friends as he ate the last of the warm and satisfying fish.

After they ate, they took to the trail toward Akeyera's kingdom again. They followed the trail until the stars were bright above them, and then they set up their camp for what they hoped would be the last time on the road. Akeyera laid her pack out for the night and stared at the stars awhile before falling asleep. Everyone woke around the same time with the bright sun warming them as they ate a small breakfast. Seafra and Jahari were in a deep conversation when they suddenly halted. At the front of the line, they saw Akeyera get off her horse and stand perfectly still as she gazed across a vast chasm that unnaturally tore their current path in two. There had been a road there at one time, and pieces of what must have been an impressively laid road were strewn everywhere.

King Demeerco, Conall, Seafra and Derek all came and stood next to Akeyera.

She stared blankly in front of her. "I remember this so differently. This is the road I used to ride down with my father to my kingdom after a long hunt. What has happened since I have been away? I fear for what we might find if the road is in this much disrepair," Akeyera said, still staring forlornly ahead.

"This is just another part of our journey together. How far is your castle from here?" Conall asked, trying to refocus their leader. They needed her.

"It is not that far. Maybe before nightfall we will reach it, depending on how far we have to go around that tear through the earth. I have this sinking feeling that somehow I am responsible for this. What if I did this while under Irenen's control?"

"Let us get to your castle and then search for the answers." Conall hoped this would draw Akeyera back to the task at hand.

Akeyera didn't know why, but today, when they were so close to ending their long journey, she wanted to quit. Just sitting down and letting everyone go on without her sounded better. As she argued with herself, she knew she could not let everyone down when they were so close to their goal.

"That is wise advice. Yes, let us ride to the castle and hope for some answers and rest there."

They started their way across the broken path. It took longer than expected since the large pieces of road awkwardly jutted out from different angles. Everyone also had to jump over the tear in the earth since the length seemed to stretch on for miles, like someone intended for no one to ever enter the land again. The chasm made a slight howling sound as the wind blew across it. Conall peeked into the gaping crevasse as he leapt across it. He could see no end, just a deep darkness, and when the wind stopped, the low howl continued. To Conall it sounded sad, and he wondered what was down there.

They continued until they could see a castle standing in a haze at a distance to the left of them. As they gazed at the sight before them, a mist rose from a sea far ahead. Ruins had fallen here and there, but a large gray castle near the sunny sea seemed untouched. The landscape was not only unfamiliar, it didn't make sense. Where they stood, snow sprinkled the ground, and their breaths came out in little puffs. The cold winter forest seemed to tumble down the steep side of the mountain, moving through the seasons in the leaves to haphazardly greet the water below.

Akeyera turned to all of them. "I remember this place." With a grin, she said, "Welcome to the land I grew up calling the Forgotten Kingdom."

Then an unexpected sight appeared as they continued forward, to the right of them, hidden behind large ancient pine trees, stood a quaint cabin with smoke comfortably making its way into the sky through a brick chimney. Akeyera silently made the signal to draw their weapons and seek cover in the surrounding bushes. She cautiously made her way to the door, her hand on the hilt of her sword, unsure of what would greet her. She wondered if the quest to her kingdom had all been in vain.

12

A KNOCK

Corbett and Ida slept comfortably in the hand-made wooden chairs they had been talking in. Ida dreamed of the day Irenen's soldier came knocking on her door. The knocking in her dream became louder and louder until she startled awake. She sat silently for a moment. Everything seemed unfamiliar, and her heart stilled a beat. The knock came again.

She shook Corbett, whispering fervently, "Corbett, somebody is at the door."

Corbett startled awake, a little disoriented. He looked around the room and heard a knock. He quickly grabbed his hunting blade. "Ida, get under the table."

"Let me help you. I can fight, too."

Corbett responded to her request with a stern look. She quietly obeyed, not happy about it.

In all his years living in this strange unpredictable land, he had learned to be cautious of any visitor. "Who is it?" he yelled. He feared Irenen had found him after all these years of hiding.

A woman's voice answered him. "My name is Akeyera. My fellow travelers and I are in need of rest. This is the first home we have come across on our journey. Will you aid us, or must we move on?"

This took Corbett by surprise. A woman's voice? He peeked out the closest window. A lone woman stood on his porch step. Cautiously, he opened the door, blade drawn. A tall blond woman stood before him. "You look safe enough but I can never be sure of people who travel through this area. Are you working for Irenen?" At this question he thought for sure he would see a cold look in her eyes.

She looked wearily back at him. "No I am not. I have journeyed far and if you will not grant us rest we will be quickly on our way." She turned to leave.

Her response surprised Corbett. "Wait, I will allow you to stay here a night because of how you answered my question and then you must be on your way. Like I said, I have to be cautious. Please wait here a moment. I need to grab my jacket, and then you can follow me to where you will be staying."

He sneaked a quick sideways look at Ida, who lay under the table, with a serious look on her face, holding a hunting bow. As he paused to lock the door, he could hear hushed breathing in the stillness of the forest around them. He slyly rested his hand on his blade.

Two men approached from the nearby bushes and came to stand near the blond woman.

"Is this all of your party? They must be loud breathers, then," Corbett said as he scanned the area, a little perplexed that his hearing had failed him.

There was a long, silent pause as the two of them stared at each other, trying to read what the other was planning to do, if anything.

"No, there are more. It is safe!" she yelled, and the rest of her party appeared. As a large number of people emerged from the forest, Corbett could not believe his eyes. There behind this stranger, a man emerged from the trees that looked similar to his friend Dem, but it had been so many years that he could not be positive that it was him.

"Dem?" he whispered. The door behind him made a faint squeak.

Akeyera immediately put her hand on the hilt of her sword, staring at the stranger before her. She slowly raised her blade and held it pointed at his heart, not wavering in the slightest as she waited for his response.

Corbett felt as if he were standing in a waking dream, ignoring the woman before him. Maybe he had been injured in his rescue of Ida, or his mind had gone into shock at the threat that stood before him. He stared for a moment longer in the direction of the man that looked uncannily like Dem, just slightly older and now with a scar across his face.

"This can't be. All my prayers in the dark nights must have been heard. I used to be the king's craftsman so many years ago."

"King Demeerco, would you please come here? Our newfound acquaintance would like to meet you." Akeyera kept her hand steady, not trusting the stranger before her.

The king had seen who came out of the quaint, inviting cabin, but knew it was impossible: Corbett had died. As he walked toward the two, he wondered who this stranger really was.

"This is impossible. You look to be an older version of a dear friend of mine who has long since passed. It is impossible—you could not be Corbett. If you are Corbett, what was the last thing you made for my kingdom?"

Corbett could barely contain the tears welling up in his eyes. This was Dem, no doubt. What had brought him here, he could only guess. He could feel the electricity building around them again, just as the first time they met. This encounter would be what they needed to reunite the isolated kingdoms, and he knew by the fact that he stood before Dem with a weary group of travelers that Irenen had done something terrible.

Gathering his thoughts, he looked directly at the king. "I built you a table, but not just any table. A table to fit at least sixty people, if not more, on each side. It had an oak tree in the center with rose petal leaves, and the legs—"

At that moment, King Demeerco gave Corbett a huge hug. Akeyera rested her sword, the threat obviously subdued.

"I don't know how you came back from the dead, and I am sure the story is one worth listening to. Oh, friend, how I have missed you. To think of happier times, I can't believe it is you."

"And I can't believe it is you. I never thought this day would come. Only in my dreams did I hope for such a reunion," Corbett said thoughtfully.

Ida had her ear to the barely open door the entire time, straining to listen to what was happening. She could see an outline of Corbett. As she peered around, a man came into view, and a gasp caught in Ida's throat. There stood Dem like a ghost from her past. She disregarded Corbett's caution and shoved open the cabin door.

Akeyera put her hand on her sword. Ida hesitated a moment in the open doorway as she gazed at the unfamiliar face of Akeyera.

"Akeyera, it is all right," King Demeerco said. "I know this woman. This is Ida, Corbett's wife."

Ida moved past Akeyera, with authority, and walked briskly to Dem and embraced him. "Oh, Dem, I thought I would never see you again or Corbett for that matter. It is almost too much for my mind to handle."

At that moment, Conall broke cover, not able to contain himself any longer. "Mother?"

Ida recognized that voice. Could it be? She gazed at the line of trees. Oh, it was. She ran toward the young man who also ran toward her. "Oh, Conall, I thought I would never see you again." She pulled away and gazed up into his face, which she quickly noted she had never had to look up at his face before. "You look so different, but your voice...I know it like I know my own. What a happy day this is."

"I guess the element of surprise is no longer needed, friend," Dem said with a slap on Corbett's back.

"Just like old times, huh, Dem?" Corbett replied, rubbing his shoulder with a smile on his lips.

The other men and women broke through the tree line. Titus hung back with Juliana—she was still unpredictable.

"I have changed my mind and you can all stay longer than one night." Corbett said this with a big smile. "The Forgotten Kingdom has plenty of resources and shelter. You can stay here as long as you need. Not sure what you need for that dog there, but everyone else I am pretty sure we can make comfortable."

Seafra meandered to where Corbett was standing and sat right in front of him. "I am no dog, sir. My name is Seafra."

"Oh, um...I guess I have not met someone quite like you. My apologies, Seafra. My name is Corbett, and welcome to what I like to call the Forgotten Kingdom. It seemed an appropriate name for this place as I could never seem to locate its actual name."

"I know the name," Akeyera said hesitantly, not sure if she wanted to share it again.

"You do? How do you know this?" Corbett inquired quizzically.

"I am the princess from the castle that still seems to stand untouched by time over there. This is what I used to know as the unique land of Tumbling Timberland, but the Forgotten Kingdom seems a much better name at present."

"I have never heard a more apt name. The timber does indeed seem to be tumbling through the seasons all the way down to the sea below. It is an odd sight that I still have not grown accustomed to," Corbett said.

Ida interrupted the moment with her excitement. "Oh, I can't believe this is happening. Conall standing here with Dem in what is a wonderful place called the Forgotten Kingdom. I feel as if someone is missing though, Ethel, where is she? Is she in the back of the line there? That woman looks kind of like her but older. I have so much to share with her, where is she?"

Everyone became silent at the mention of Ethel's name.

"Ida, Ethel is—"

"Dem, I am sorry to interrupt. We can discuss Ethel later. At this time, our people need rest, food, and a place to stay for a while." Akeyera could tell by Ida's complexion that she was not quite well and feared the news of what happened to Ethel might shock her somehow in her obviously weakened state.

"You must excuse my hosting skills," Corbett said. "I have never had to host in the kingdom before or, as a matter of fact, host at all in these past lonely years. Yes, I agree. Let me assist you weary travelers before we get lost in conversation that can wait until later. Let us make you a place you can stay for a good while."

As they began to walk past Corbett's cabin, Akeyera waved her hand for the others to follow. Just a short distance away, along an overgrown path, an old barracks sat empty, its roof somewhat intact. Akeyera gazed at it, hoping yet another memory would come fleeting through her mind, but nothing stirred.

"Here is where you can stay. It doesn't look like much, but it is quite large. I have had plenty of time to keep working on my woodworking skills here in this old barracks." Corbett unlocked the heavy wooden doors.

As their eyes adjusted to the dim light inside, a large room greeted them with hallways sprouting off either side. A massive fireplace with a beautiful rock mantle draped across its sides took center stage. A few holes were visible through the rock walls as the sun peeked through, making the dust dance in the light.

"Corbett, this will work great," Akeyera said while scanning the large room.

"I hope it will. This is the main room, which I have spent the most time on. The fireplace is in working condition. This hallway to the left has about twelve separate rooms in livable condition, each with a bed, but you will have to make your own mattresses, as they have deteriorated over time. That doorway near the fireplace leads into a nice kitchen and this hallway to the right leads to a few more rooms that could be used as bedrooms and two other large rooms, one that is an armory and one a storage area with supplies I have gathered. If you would follow me, I can help you gather the supplies you need."

"Corbett, thanks. This is going to work for us. I am going to stay behind and start telling people where to set up so we can have a place to sleep before the night comes upon the surrounding land."

"Oh, I have not been paying attention to the time. Yes, I don't mind at all, Akeyera. It looks like Dem has recruited a few more to come assist us. That will work perfectly."

Akeyera started the task of setting up not just camp but life for a while in the large room. She knew they would all need some time to recover and formulate a plan of rescue. She also wanted to explore the surrounding areas to see what she could remember.

"Dem, I cannot believe you are walking beside me with my wife, Ida, whom I thought I would never see again."

Ida walked in quiet concentration next to Conall and desperately wanted to know about Ethel. She fought within herself to not blurt out her questions but knew that now was not the time to ask. They passed a few rooms and other hallways and finally stopped at another large wooden door.

"Here is everything I think you will need," Corbett said, opening large closet doors.

The shelves were lined with blankets, clothes, shoes, and an assortment of miscellaneous items.

"Wow, it looks like you have been resourceful with your time here, Corbett. Everyone, grab as many blankets and pillows as you can. We can always come back if we need more," Dem said.

As they walked back down the hallway, the smell of hot herbs pricked their nostrils. In the main room, a warm fire greeted them. People sat around different tables, eating bowls of something that smelled delicious.

"Dem, it looks as if your group is making themselves at home already. I will let you join them. Ida and I will retire for the night and see you in the morning, even though I want nothing more than to ask you many questions, which I am sure you have some for us too. Good night, Dem."

"Good night, Corbett. See you in the morning, and, yes, I have many questions as well. We will save them for when we are all rested."

Ida slowly opened one sleepy eye and stared out one of the cabin widows. The sunrays were just barely visible, yet someone knocked on their door. She felt as if she had just fallen asleep, the excitement of the day still coursed through her veins. "Honey, someone is—"

"I have a feeling I know who it is." Corbett stretched and yawned. "Our first early morning guest is..." He swung open his front door, and the smell of sleeping woods greeted him. "Dem. I guessed correctly. Good early morning to you."

"Just like old times, right, Corbett? I couldn't stand waiting to see you any longer."

"Come on in and make yourself comfortable. Ida and I will get dressed and be right out."

As Dem sat on a comfortable rocking chair, his eyes scanned the room. This cabin was beautiful in a rustic way. Corbett's woodwork could be seen throughout, still talented. He sat gazing at a small bookshelf near him and smiled as a familiar title greeted his eyes: *The Kingdom of Shadow and Sun*. It had been many years since that joyous morning. Such a fond memory he thought, happy to have Corbett and Ida in his life once again.

Ida started a pot of water over the fire while Corbett began preparing some eggs. The three of them chatted comfortably like they had only been away from each other for a few days rather than many years.

"This is fun. Sounds like the others are up." A low murmur of voices could be heard in the distance. "I did make extra just in case anyone else decides to join us, but I won't have enough if everyone decides to squeeze into our quaint little kitchen," Ida said as she peered into the sizzling egg pan.

"That was wise because it looks like Akeyera and Conall just walked past your window."

Corbett saw them, too, and opened the front door before they could knock. "Good morning. Come on in. Sit down, and we will bring breakfast to you."

"It looks like you were expecting us. Thank you, Corbett," Akeyera said with a courteous smile.

After the pleasantries had been exchanged and the food served, an awkward silence fell into the room.

Dem knew what needed or rather who needed to be discussed. "I think it should be said now. We need to tell Corbett and Ida the truth about my daughter and Ida's adopted daughter Ethel. I know it is early, but you need to know why we are here. I am going to tell you plainly. She has joined forces with my brother, Irenen."

Shock registered on Ida's face. "How? Why? She would never do such a thing!" A few tears slipped down her cheeks.

Akeyera took a moment before speaking not wanting to upset Ida even more. "We can only guess what forced her to join sides with Irenen. What we need to do is figure out a plan to rescue her. I escaped that dark kingdom. Juliana escaped that kingdom, and so have a few others. So there is hope for Ethel that she can, too, even though she may not be who she was the last time we saw her. First, we need to recover here a little while longer. We are weak at the moment. Plus it will give us time to formulate the right plan of attack." Akeyera said this hoping that more time would aid her in remembering her past.

"I agree with you, Akeyera. That needs to be the start of the plan. We can discuss the next part in detail later. For now, let us continue to make this our home," Conall said.

"Juliana was captured? Wow, we have missed so much," Ida said quietly.

"My poor daughter. What could Irenen have done to her to make her choose his side?"

"Ida," Corbett said, "don't let yourself dwell on it too long. No good will come from that. Instead think of how we can be helping her."

"You are right. We can be helping her, but how? I know nothing of strategy or war, but I am good at seeing needs that need to be fulfilled. I will help in any way I can without getting in the way," Ida said with a determined tone and stomp of her foot.

"We will need all the help we can get. Our numbers are not as great as they were when we first entered Irenen's kingdom, but we still have great power in the group that we have here. What we need—" A knock interrupted Akeyera.

Corbett opened the door. Derek entered the room, holding what looked like a variety of fruit and fresh biscuits. "I thought all of you might like some brain food before you start coming up with plans of what we do next. I know most of you well enough to know you will work the day away without remembering to eat or taking the time to prepare something for yourselves. This should help all of you stay focused. I will not be staying. There is plenty to do in the main building. Please enjoy."

"Thank you, Derek."

"You are welcome."

Ida reached out and held Conall's hand. "I am worried for Ethel. Maybe I did the wrong thing by sending you both into the forest."

"Mother, you did the right thing. Don't worry. We will find a way to rescue Ethel."

"I hope we will."

They sat around the quaint table, enjoying the fresh fruit.

"Since we are talking about rescuing my sister, I think we should just march in there and get her. Walk right up to the door—"

"I appreciate your bravery," Akeyera said, "but I don't think that would be the wisest idea. We may have injured their troops, but they still have great man power if that is what you want to call those creatures. No, I think we will have to come up with a much more secret approach. I think I may know an unexpected passage that is located at the bottom of an ancient well." A faint image of a tunnel and well revealed themselves slowly to Akeyera's memory.

"How do you know of this?" Corbett asked.

"This is my lost kingdom, and I am its princess. I guess, sadly now, the queen as I don't see how any could have survived this destruction around us. I must have been gone longer than I thought. To me, it seemed only a year, but to gaze at this once fertile land, it has to have been years since I left this place. There is a distant side to me that hums with lost memories of better times here, and yet I can't shake off the feeling that I am responsible for this somehow."

"Responsible how?" Corbett asked.

"That, I am not quite sure of. As I remember my past, I will do my best to share it with you. Would you like to search out the location of the well with me?"

"Yes, that sounds interesting," Corbett replied.

"I vaguely remember where it is. When it went dry many years ago, my father let me go with him to explore the bottom. He wanted to see if he could find the problem. When we reached the bottom, we found a tunnel with an old map showing it connecting with a few other wells throughout the land. I remember my father being shocked that a map carving had survived all the years of water. He had no idea that his ancient kingdom contained such a secret. He explored the tunnels a few times until finally he came home after being gone for a few days and said he had found the first connection. I remember being excited to hear about what had been discovered and waiting for him to continue sharing. He never did. I asked what he had found, and he said a dark place that no one needs to see. The exploration stopped after that, and a new well was dug."

Corbett helped Ida with the last of the dishes, speaking to Akeyera while he washed. "I think I may know where you are talking about, but that area is the most damaged. Darkness seems to want to congregate there. It is the one area that has been the hardest to keep maintained from being overtaken by wild things. It is past the orchard, so we could have a few others come with us to gather plenty of fruit. You will find that this kingdom has been enchanted or maybe this is how it has always been. Seasons pass normally here on the edge, but as we near the heart of...what did you call it?...the Forgotten Kingdom, you will find the air never gets cold, which is why there is a beautiful continuous orchard." Corbett said this with a wave of his hand toward the castle.

"I believe that is the way it has always been here. Although I seem to remember that the seasons fluctuated less on the edge of the kingdom, which seemed much farther away than the cabin you are residing in. But that memory could be wrong. I do, however, remember eating fresh fruit year-round. Funny what the mind remembers."

While Akeyera spoke, Conall walked over to the others in the main building. He gathered about seven people to pick fruit and perhaps hunt if needed. He did not want to waste time.

"Let's go," Akeyera said.

"Ida, would you like to come or stay here?" Corbett asked while putting an arm around his wife's waist.

"I would like to stay here and help in the main building. I still do not feel quite myself."

"That is fine." Corbett kissed her before they left.

Conall watched the back of Akeyera's blond head as they began to walk and wondered what she was remembering. "Akeyera, when you were under Irenen's control, did you ever remember your kingdom? I want some hope of Ethel possibly remembering us."

"Hmm...let me think." She paused, trying hard to remember her dark time at Irenen's castle. "My first memories of my kingdom awakened in me when Irenen had assigned an older man to extract light from me. After months of him already being under Irenen's watchful eyes, Irenen asked me if I knew him. I remember thinking how odd of Irenen to ask me that. I did not know the tortured man that stood before me that day."

"How long had you been with Irenen by then?" Conall asked curiously.

"I had felt that I had been in Irenen's service for years and knew no one outside the castle walls. As I stood there, that tortured man whispered, 'Akeyera?' A flash through my mind happened as I stared at him—of him full of laughter, holding my hand as a child. He wore a crown in that image. Then I remember not knowing at the time why I did it, but I opened his cage and grabbed his hand, and without speaking to him, I led him to an entrance that not many people in the kingdom had used since I had been there. As I handed him a few items I knew he would need for survival and soothing ointment for his injuries that I knew would scar him for a lifetime, he whispered my name again. 'Akeyera, do you not recognize me?' I told him no, and the sadness that ripped through his body into his oddly colored blue eyes was visibly seen." Akeyera paused for a moment as emotions welled up inside her.

"Is that when you started to remember again? I bet it felt as if you were a stranger in your own mind. Having encountered Irenen, I know firsthand how he can warp a person's mind," Corbett said.

"Yes, that moment awoke something in my mind that Irenen had tried to erase. I started remembering bits and pieces from that moment forward. I did not remember much detail of my kingdom until we started our journey here. Glimpses and pieces have drifted into my mind—me as a child holding my father's hand, who I realize was the man I released from Irenen's kingdom so many years ago." Akeyera said this not sure how the others would react.

"What, how can that be? You said you didn't know that strange man you released," Conall said, shocked.

"I only just remembered this, and I hope he finds us here. He is the man who assisted us in the woods before we attempted to rescue Ethel. I hope as we are here for a few weeks that anyone we may have left behind during the attack will show up here. I have many questions. My mind still seems locked when it comes to my past, which may be protecting me from great sadness. I am grateful for this so we can stay focused on the task. I am sorry I didn't know my father the day we tried to rescue Ethel. I am sure he was unsure of what that information would do to me and wanted to wait for the right timing."

"Wow, your father a king. I hope he does find us soon. Strange to think he stood there among us and didn't tell you or any of us who he was. He must have had his reasons," Corbett said thoughtfully. "I do have a question that has been rolling around in my head for a while."

"And what is your question?" Akeyera asked.

"That day we found you, you carried an odd-looking stone. What was that?"

Akeyera paused, unsure if she wanted to share that piece of dangerous information. She decided it would be better for Conall to know. "I stole that from Irenen's room. He had dug it up in secret tunnels below the Wooded Kingdom while I was in his control. Before I escaped, I stole it, knowing that it would delay whatever he had been working on. I knew from his mutterings that it contained a great light within it, but he could not seem to break it."

"Where is it?" Dem asked suspiciously.

"Here with me." Akeyera opened her leather-bound case that she carried everywhere with her and held the stone out for all to see.

Dem reached out and touched it. The glowing orb seemed to hum happily at his touch. "It's making noise. Curious." He stared intently into the orb, hoping a secret would reveal itself, but nothing happened.

"Yes, it does that on occasion. I had hoped you would know more about it. It seems almost as if it is living," Akeyera said.

"I can tell you this: if anyone in my kingdom knows about this, they have kept it a secret. I bet we could find out in the book my father gave me, which is still in my kingdom unless Irenen has burned it to the ground. Please continue to keep the orb safe as you have been doing." Dem said this while still gazing at the mysterious orb, which began a low singsong type of hum.

"I will continue to protect it until we know what to do with it. I am beginning to recognize this area. I believe the well is right around—"

13

THE PASSAGE

"Hey, I found it." The thought of the humming orb quickly drifted away as Conall's mind became occupied with the next task. He stood near the edge of what used to be a nice, large well. The crumbling bricks lay on the ground with vines weaving a thick web, almost obscuring the entire well from view. He began gingerly removing the vines, trying not to fall into the slowly growing, dark hole. A hollow wind blew up from somewhere deep. He gazed into the hole and saw nothing but darkness. The noise made him shiver.

"Wow, Conall, thank you. I do remember this place, sitting on that rock over there while my mother and father lay in the grass reading a book. It's such a strange feeling to remember something that feels like a memory that belongs to someone else." Akeyera peered down the dark hole. "I was thinking we would climb down, but it looks like that may be difficult with the erosion."

"I think I have an idea. Here, let us lower this lantern down first to see how deep it is." Corbett quickly tied a rope to a lit lantern and slowly lowered it down.

It felt as if it would never reach the bottom, but then they all began to see the small light flickering above some dirt. Gently, he set down the lantern without knocking it over. Conall didn't wait to discuss his plan. He had eyed the width of the hole and the depth. He jumped right in.

It was so sudden, no one responded right away.

"Conall!" Dem shouted, his heart pounding rapidly.

He ignored the shout. He was tired of talking about everything first, and he knew this would work. His heart thumped loudly, and the wind rushed passed his ears. He opened his wings, which allowed him a slower speed. He hit the bottom more at a hard jump, misjudging the exit hole and the depth to the ground. The air rushed out of him as he hit the ground, and he lost his balance and knocked over the lantern. He was in utter darkness.

The others watched as the light went out. "Conall, can you hear us? Conall!"

Conall sat on the cold, damp ground trying to get his bearings. The darkness seemed impenetrable expect for the yawing mouth of light above him. He could hear faint voices above. "Can you lower another lantern?" he shouted as loud as he could. He hadn't thought of bringing any supplies down with him. Conall's voice echoed off the brick as it traveled up the well.

"Shh...I think I hear him." Akeyera could make out what he was saying but barely. "Tie that other lantern to the rope, and lower it slowly."

They waited a few anxious moments, and then they could make out Conall holding the lantern.

"I think I should go down to do a little exploring," Akeyera said. "I don't think it wise to leave Conall down there by himself."

"I agree. But let's set up a few ropes here so you can go down more easily." Dem helped tie a rope around Akeyera's tiny waist for safety measures.

As she peered down at the flickering lantern below, a shiver of dread crept up her spine. She focused her mind, knowing that feeling such an emotion had to be something from her past. She grabbed a rope and made her way down the well more gracefully than Conall did.

Conall stood and watched, and as Akeyera came closer, she punched his arm. He stepped to the side confused.

"Ow! Why did you punch me?" Conall said.

"Because you could have jumped down into a trap or been seriously injured. We talk about what we are doing next to avoid things like this. If you do something like this again, you will be confined to the barracks! Do you understand?"

"Yes, Akeyera," Conall said sheepishly. "I couldn't wait for any more talking about what we were going to do next or who was going to go down. Talk, talk, talk—I feel like that is all we have been doing. I am itching to rescue my sister. I will admit though that my plan didn't quite work the way I had hoped. I am a little sore, but I know that is my own fault. I am sorry."

"Apology accepted. Let's light this other lantern and leave it on the ground so we can find our way back. I seem to remember the map being somewhere right around here, near one of the maintenance entrances. Ah, here it is."

They stood in front of an ancient carving of a network of tunnels etched into the stone wall. The damp, whining wind made the dust swirl at their feet.

"The water must have been gone from this place for quite a while. Looks like somebody put some marks here on the map where the water used to come from," Conall said.

Little blue dots started from a place on the map and faded until they reached where they were standing, on a big purple gash on the map that also matched a spot on the ground where they stood.

Akeyera held up the lantern in either direction. The light fell short on either side. "I think this will be the best way to enter Irenen's kingdom again, but it looks like we could also access the Wooded Kingdom here." Akeyera pointed her finger on the cold, hard map. "This must be a type of servicing area, which would allow us a way around the water that we may encounter. Maybe we could recruit some more people from King Dem's kingdom. It looks like a long way to travel by foot."

Conall stretched out his wings. "I can think of another way to travel."

"Hmm...that is a possibility. We should set up a few small traps down here to make sure these tunnels are truly empty. Any darkness like this makes me wary of what is lurking behind the corners. Then we can gather a few men and do some scouting trips before we decide on how exactly to get Ethel."

Another cloud of dust blew past them, stronger this time, and went up the well shaft.

"Odd that there is a strong wind down here. There has to be another hole not too far off. Here, Akeyera, you can go first. I will be right behind you."

They assisted each other with tying off their ropes, Conall noting that Akeyera was quite shapely. He blushed in the dark, hoping she didn't notice.

"I am ready!" Akeyera shouted, pulling on the rope. She began to slowly rise.

Conall watched her graceful form for a moment, blushing yet again, but in the confines of the dark tunnel, he let his blush rise. Making sure his rope was taught, he reached down for the last lantern, and a stronger gust blew past him, blowing out the light. He pulled hard on his rope, a feeling of unease growing in the pit of his stomach. He began to rise, but it didn't feel fast enough. He put his hand on his sword and swung himself to one side of the well.

Akeyera saw Conall's rope go slack and turned around, thinking he was still on the ground messing around. Complete darkness greeted her eyes. "Conall, this isn't funny! Conall!" She reached out and pulled on his rope, but no resistance met her. She pulled it quickly only to find the end covered in a thick black slime. "Lower me down! Conall, I am coming. I said lower me down!"

She emerged angrily from the top of the well. "We have to go down there. Conall is—"

"We know. We saw something. Not sure what, but it went after Conall's rope. Perhaps there is another entrance. Conall is smart. He will survive whatever comes his way," Dem said, concern etched in his features.

"I believe there is. Follow me this way." Akeyera began running the way the wind had been coming down in the tunnel. She ran quickly, forgetting the others.

14

EMPTY TEARS

The warm drops of liquid fell in slow, steady streams. Ethel opened her eyes only to find they were wet again. She had dreamed once again about that strange boy she encountered only a few months ago. As on that day and many after, in her dreams her eyes leaked with water. She had asked a few servants in her castle of the meaning of the water, and they always replied, "That is just the way of eyes."

She didn't feel content. Her mind wrestled with the simple answer as she awoke with wet eyes yet again. She needed to get her mind off this. She walked onto her balcony, which reached out beyond the precipice that the castle stood on, and gazed at the dark rolling hills that lay below her. The few remaining sticks of once large trees swayed in the forceful wind below, but

one tree always stood out to her. Tucked away in a corner at the edge of her soon-to-be kingdom, a twinkle of
color reflected in the filtered sunlight. She had noticed
it before and always intended to ride out and get rid
of whatever it was, but every time she set out to do so,
something stopped her. Today would be the day.

"Ethel, sorry to bother you this morning, but the
king is asking for you."

Ethel didn't feel the need to respond. She felt empty
inside today. Her mind still flitted to that bit of color,
and she wanted to wipe it out. Irenen had not passed
away after being stabbed when that strange boy had
tried to take her with him the day of the battle. Everyone
in the kingdom was working hard to repair the dam-
age and locate the people who had done this. Irenen
knew the people, she knew it, but he refused to tell her
anything. She stomped her feet harder as she walked
in protest over the way Irenen treated her. Her mind
drifted to thoughts of Irenen's wound, which was grave.
She smirked. The sound of voices gently caressed the
hallway.

Irenen's voice was barely audible, and a few words
drifted out the cracks of the worn door. "Demeerco
knows the bush...golden...long life...must find the orb..."

She heard just enough to spark her curiosity, and
she quickly pushed the door open to make it seem as if
she had just arrived, not caring if she startled the sick
king. "Hello, Irenen. Anything I need to know about?"

She thought perhaps the two standing before her
would divulge what they were discussing, but they
stared blankly back at her. She felt a detachment as she

stared down at her father. Somehow he looked oddly unfamiliar. A thought wiggled itself in her mind: if he should pass, she felt she would go on with life much as it was except she would become queen. "Queen" had a nice ring to it. More power would be nice, and perhaps long life would be included in her reign as queen. She would need to discover what they had been talking about. To be the grandest and most powerful queen any had seen—that is what she wanted. She noticed Irenen's lips moving, but she had not been listening until now when he mentioned her mother.

"...foolish I had been at seeing what lie before me in that clearing and choosing to pursue your mother instead. If I had raised you like I wanted to, things would be much different," Irenen said through wheezing breaths.

She yawned, growing bored of his hanging on to life. "What are you babbling about? Pursuing my mother? Seeing something in a clearing? Oh, never mind. I don't care enough to hear your answer."

Irenen stared blankly through Ethel with his dark eyes. *What had he created?* He felt thirsty and reached out toward Demerell, his faithful servant, who stood at the head of the bed, giving Irenen the sweetest-smelling purple liquid that Ethel had yet smelled. Ethel closed her eyes savoring the smell, which made her realize how parched she actually was. What a waste to be giving that to Irenen. She did not treat Demerell with disdain, for he along with a few others had proven to her that they were useful to the kingdom. "Demerell, is there any more of that?"

Demerell looked into the cup. The last few drops sloshed on its cloudy bottom. He passed a sour look down at Irenen. Irenen's clammy pale hand shot up and forcefully grabbed the cup, passing the last few drops of liquid into his always parched mouth, gazing at Ethel as he did so.

Irenen had Ethel's attention. "My plan did not work. My life was not supposed to be this way. I wanted to be sitting in my brother's throne room with you by my side, conquering the land as far as we could reach, and I see my folly." A single tear slid down Irenen's ghostly pale skin. "I should've listened to my father. Power is not what I thought it would be. I understand what he was trying to tell me the day I killed him. Ethel, I...I..." Irenen slid into a sleep. Demerell shook him, but he did not stir and beads of sweat formed on Irenen's brow.

Ethel seethed inside with anger until it burst out. "How could you say that? Power is everything! I don't care about your regrets. This kingdom will be great, and I will make it great!"

She stormed out of the room to grab her beautiful sword that she had found lying on the side of a dried-up riverbed. Its ruby hilt felt comfortable in her hand—its blade a thing of dark beauty. She had often wondered who would toss such a valuable object away like that. It seemed as if it had been made for her. After she took care of Irenen once and for all, she would grill Demerell for information on what they had been discussing before she entered. She paused for a moment to wipe water from her eyes once again, and a twinge resonated in her heart as an image of a white castle surfaced from deep inside her as her hand brushed across the ruby hilt. "I will forget you, memory or whatever this is. I have things to accomplish," she whispered as she stormed toward Irenen's door.

"Demerell!" she shouted, slashing madly at the empty air in Irenen's room as she burst through the door.

The room was bare. Demerell and Irenen were missing. At the sound of her shouting, others came running. They waited to speak until her anger had subsided. They were used to Irenen's outbursts, but Lady Ethel was far more unpredictable and cruel.

"What is it, Lady Ethel?" Wren asked.

The voice made her pause. She caught her breath and shouted at all of them, pointing her sword. "Find them now!"

She went to her room and stood angrily on the balcony, wishing her gaze would destroy that happy, glinting weeping willow in the distance. The moon shone brightly on Irenen's kingdom below her, and hours passed with no word of where her father or Demerell had disappeared to. She began to nod off as she leaned on the balcony, dreaming scattered dreams of that boy again and succulent purple liquid. Screams echoed in her mind, but she couldn't place them in her dream. She started awake as one of the servants, Wren, lightly touched her arm.

"Lady Ethel, I am sorry. We have searched much of the night but to no avail. They are gone—no trace of them anywhere. Here, let me help you into your bed."

She allowed the assistance into her bed as her sleepy body seemed to float happily through the air. "Wren?"

"Yes, my lady," she replied as she tucked Ethel into her bed.

"Don't call me lady anymore. I am your queen. Inform the others!" She rolled over and drifted into her first peaceful sleep in many weeks.

Wren gazed down at the beautiful Ethel, wondering about her reign, not daring to run, for fear of what she would do if she found any of them. Wren walked to her quarters to tell the others of the news, unsure of what the rule of Queen Ethel would bring.

15

RUN

Conall fell hard on the cold ground. His eyes adjusting to the dark quickly, he was in trouble, he began to run in the direction the wind had come just moments ago. The feeling of pursuit pounded in his chest, and he came crashing down to the ground, rolling quickly to his side. He could not see his mysterious attacker but continued to run toward a pinpoint of light that was not far ahead. It looked like a break in the once sealed water tunnel. As he neared, he could see it was a large break. Large enough for one of Irenen's creatures, he thought. He grabbed his sword, put his hand on his ring to blind whatever pursued him, and swung out blindly as he flew to the opening of daylight. A bloodcurdling scream ripped through whatever he had struck and continued to follow him into the light. He quickly stood on the edge of the old tunnel system and waited to stab what-ever would exit behind him.

Everything stilled around him, the air felt as if it weighed him down as he waited. Slowly, a huge beast began to emerge from the tunnel. Conall stabbed at it once again, its beating heart clearly visible through its leathery clear-colored skin. It screamed as Conall's strike landed a heavy blow on its massive skull. It fell to the ground, black ooze seeping from its wounds. Conall stared at the strange creature, his sword dripping with blackness. He suddenly felt weary, and he collapsed onto a fallen pillar at some old entrance.

Akeyera picked up her pace as she heard a horrible sound that didn't seem human. Her heart felt as if it would pound out of her chest as she ran. She rounded a slight bend, and there, next to an old fallen pillar, sat Conall, his wings spotted with black. "Conall!"

Conall turned toward the voice, noticing the crea-ture's black blood speckling his body. He tried to move toward Akeyera, but his legs were weak. He continued to lean on a pillar for support.

"Here, have some water, and sit and rest. Are you injured?" Akeyera fussed over Conall for only a moment before she realized what she was doing. She had not cared this much about someone for a long time, or if so, she could not remember. She quickly stood and composed herself before anyone noticed her actions.

"I don't think so, but this black blood is actually starting to hurt my skin. Would you help me walk to that stream over there?" He pointed weakly.

The others finally appeared around a corner, out of breath.

"Dem, could you help me?" Akeyera asked. "The rest of you, keep your eye on that creature. I don't trust that it's really dead."

Dem and Akeyera helped Conall lie down in the peaceful, cool stream. The thick blood took a little while to loosen, but finally every last spot of it was gone.

"There must be a poison of some sort in that creature's blood. I feel much better." Conall had bruises everywhere the blood had touched him. Having washed off, he gingerly made his way back to the creature.

They all stood staring at the strange creature. Corbett grabbed a stick and poked its leathery clear hide. A red spot formed under its skin, quickly turning black. "What is this creature—one of Irenen's?"

"I actually am not sure. I don't think this is one of Irenen's. I think perhaps it is a more ancient creature awakened by whatever happened here so long ago. I think to be on the safe side we should try to pull it out of the tunnel and set it on fire. I just don't trust that it is truly dead," Akeyera said, keeping a wary eye on the creature.

They began the task of throwing ropes around it, trying not to touch it. They pulled hard, and it moved slightly off the old tunnel. They pulled again, and it came crashing down, fully resting on the ground, its head falling to the side so its razor-sharp teeth glistened in the sun.

"Conall, you are lucky. I think that inner voice of yours guided you to safety," Akeyera said.

"I feel luckier after seeing those teeth."

They pulled one last time, getting the beast into a patch of cleared soil. They started a few small fires around it. It caught on fire surprisingly fast, filling the sky with a sickly black smoke. They stood by until the last of the flames subsided.

"I wish this would have been a fire to enjoy good company around," Conall said. "I have to admit, I am getting tired of no peace."

"I know what you mean, Conall, but I think we are moving down the right path that will lead us to rescuing your sister." Akeyera patted Conall on the shoulder. "I think a plan is formulating in me despite what happened moments ago. I think we should go back to the barracks before the sun gets much closer to the horizon, and we can discuss the plan after a short rest."

Dem walked over to Conall and hugged him. "I thought I had lost you. Glad to see you are all right. You sure do remind me of myself at your age."

"Thank you, Father. Instinct took over, and I ran as fast and as hard as I could. I think talking in the barracks sounds good to me. I could use a rest before we come up with a plan of attack."

The rest of the group agreed, and they began their walk back to barracks, making sure to mark any other openings they found along the way.

As Akeyera rushed to find Conall, she hadn't noticed her leather pouch catch slightly on a low-lying dead bush. "All right, then, let us make the walk back quickly. I think those tunnels will aid us greatly in our rescue of Ethel."

Akeyera began walking. The unseen hole in her brown bag began to slowly widen until finally, with a hard thump to the ground, her precious orb fell. The loss of weight around her waist made her pause. She watched in slow motion as the orb fell to the ground and rested on a bare spot. Before she could respond, an invisible wave radiated from the orb not once but twice, only being noticed by the tremor it caused underfoot. She let out a cry of dismay as the orb slowly became absorbed by the ground it rested upon until it completely disappeared.

To their amazement, a tree began to sprout, rising quickly from the ground with iridescent leaves reflecting the sun. The ground shook once again, and they struggled to keep their footing. As the ground swayed, it started sprouting grass. They quickly made their way back to the barracks as fast as their swaying legs could carry them, leaving the mysterious tree behind them. As they passed the once forlorn-looking meadows, to their amazement cracks in the ground were disappearing. As they neared the barracks, what sounded like stone grinding on stone greeted their ears. They rounded the bend, and there stood the rest of the troop, staring blankly at the barracks. Bricks were mysteriously moving by themselves. The overgrown path had been cleared to reveal what looked like newly laid brick, and the overgrown brush had thinned to reveal a wider path that led to a glistening castle in the distance.

"What is happening, Akeyera?" Corbett shouted amid the commotion. The ground continued to sway and pitch.

"I am not sure, but it looks as if whatever enchantment enclosed this kingdom has been erased. That orb, maybe it originally came from here. It is acting like a seed for a new land, reversing the destruction that was so visible here. If the barracks are this repaired, I can only imagine what the castle must look like."

The ground came to shivering halt. The rushing wind became a calm breeze, and birds were heard for the first time outside.

Dem continued to watch in amazement as the land continued to transform. "I know we only got back a few moments ago. The earth seems to have calmed, and we should go see what the castle is like. Maybe it is a safe place for us to stay, and who knows, you may find something in there that belongs to you." As Dem spoke, the others heard and didn't wait for him to finish. They all began walking toward the castle, curiosity drawing their attention elsewhere.

"Akeyera, look!" Conall pointed toward the castle.

In the distance, what looked like a group of trees broke away from the rest and slowly made their way toward them. The closer they and the trees got to each other, the more everyone realized the trees were hundreds of people. Akeyera felt a tear slide down her cheek in recognition of the people. These were her lost friends and family, somehow frozen in time and not aging a day. She ran toward them, not caring what anyone thought, and the sea of familiar faces began to run to her, recognizing their princess. The kingdom once forgotten was again restored to its former glory. This may be just what they needed to go rescue Ethel.

"Mother! Father! How is this possible—here all of you are? The entire kingdom looks as if it has survived. I remember you. I remember this place. But Corbett has been here for years and never found any of you."

"Oh, my beautiful daughter, how we have waited for you, but there will be plenty of time for talking. I think you should introduce us to the rest of the people with you."

"Oh, of course, these are my friends and what is left of our group that set out to rescue a young woman named Ethel. This is King Demeerco of the Wooded Kingdom, and this is—"

"Dem, I thought I would never see you again." Akeyera's father interrupted her in his excitement. "I was unrecognizable the day I assisted you getting into Irenen's castle, but after that strange creature captured me here, his lair restored me. I don't think that thing intended for that to happen. But what good fortune, old buddy. With this crew, we will surely be able to get rid of your brother, Irenen, once and for all."

The king's wife reached out, patting his arm gently. "Honey, shh...we only just woke from our strange slumber."

The king's large hand engulfed his wife's. "I know, my dear. I am only anxious to restore what was obviously taken from all of us."

"It is great to see you, King Tarius, old friend," Dem said. "So much has transpired since I have seen you last. I was only a young lad when my father told me your kingdom had been lost to a growing darkness. I remember the sadness we all felt in losing such good friends.

And now here you are, not aged a day. What a story you must have. Since the sun has gone and stars now shine down on us, what do you say we walk to the barracks for a meal and discuss the joyous occasion more?"

"Ah, Dem, you are much like your father. Yes, let us continue this in warmer quarters," King Tarius said in his gruff voice.

Akeyera walked between her parents, lost in confusing emotions, wishing she could remember what had happened here but knowing that would all come in due time. They sat in the crowded barrack dining room, and happy voices filled the air as new friends were made and old friends were reunited.

"I knew one day you would recognize me again, Akeyera. I came here to rest only to be captured by a strange beast with clear skin. He dragged me down into the ground, and the last thing I remember is seeing all the people of the kingdom frozen, as they were so many years ago, inside crystals. Then the ground began to shake, and we awoke and found you standing before the castle," King Tarius said in a deep, gravelly voice.

"I am sorry that I did not recognize you sooner. I have this nagging feeling that somehow I had something to do with this destruction everywhere."

At this, King Tarius looked down at his half-eaten roll, and his wife, Queen Anna, gently patted his back. "You were not yourself, Akeyera. Irenen had come to our kingdom and became smitten with you and you with him. We knew that he was nothing like his brother, Demeerco, but you would not listen, and one day you were just gone." Akeyera stared at the table as she listened to her father speak. "I searched for you but feared leaving our kingdom for too long. Then months after we had stopped our search for you, you rode into the village on a large black steed followed by huge hairless flying beasts with oddly humanistic faces, the sight of them I have never forgotten, and at the wave of your hand, those beasts destroyed everything. They tore trees out of the ground, dug their claws through the roads. So many of them swarmed the land that it shook and swayed." Akeyera didn't want to hear any more but at the same time wanted to know what had happened, so she continued to listen. "I tried to get everyone underground to safety through the dry water tunnels, and when I thought they were all safe, I resurfaced to snatch you. But I was too late. You were not you, I shouted your name and pleaded for you to stop and you sat atop your horse smiling at me through the dust of destruction that swirled around. As I shouted, a creature snatched me into the sky in his powerful claws. That is how I ended up in Irenen's dungeon." King Tarius reached out and gently patted Akeyera's hand.

Akeyera felt ashamed as she remembered bits and pieces of what she had done. She remembered feeling love for Irenen and the anger that coursed through her when she realized he had only tricked her to get her kingdom. That anger is what she had unleashed on her beloved kingdom. "I am sorry. That feels so inadequate to say for things I have done. But—"

"Shh...no more will we talk about this. What has happened is done. We cannot go back. Although I am curious, how did this destruction begin to reverse?" King Tarius inquired.

"I carried a glowing orb in a pouch of mine that I stole from Irenen some time ago. In the hurry to get here, the orb fell out, and at the touch of the ground, it began to create all of this new life around us. How it did that and where it originally came from I am unsure, but it is here under that tree with the iridescent leaves in the distance." Akeyera pointed toward the beautiful mysterious tree that grandly stood.

"That is definitely a mystery we will want to investigate at a later time. But let us talk of now and what we need to do. I assume you are here because your quest did not go as planned. Where is the one you want to rescue? Ethel, right?"

Akeyera yawned. It was late, but she felt pushed to talk of her plan. Derek was near, laughing with Corbett. "Derek, excuse me, would you mind bringing Dem, Conall, and yourself to the table? Also Juliana and Ida if they are willing?" She only had to wait a few moments before everyone arrived and sat attentively at her table.

"I hear you have a plan." Conall smiled, gently elbowing Akeyera in the side.

"Yes, I do. With the influx of people today and the plentiful supplies, I think we should take a group down into the tunnels and see if we cannot find a hidden entrance into the Dark Kingdom. A simple plan, I know, but it will work because I know Irenen knows nothing of the tunnels. We would be better prepared, too, if we should encounter any more creatures. We would send a scouting party first and work from there. What do all of you think?"

Everyone around the table looked at each other, glimmers of excitement in their eyes. "We think it sounds great!" A shout rose not only from their table but from everyone surrounding them.

"Here, here," the rest of them chimed in.

16

FOUND

"Do you have a crush on Akeyera?" Seafra asked. "What are you talking about?" Conall focused on sharpening some arrows, trying to hide his blushing face from Seafra.

"You know what I am talking about. I was only curious. I think she likes you too if that eases your embarrassment at all."

"You do? Do you think anyone else notices? Is it that obvious?"

"No, not really. Your father might notice, but he is pretty focused on Juliana's recovery to notice too many extra things. I won't say anything, but maybe when things calm down, you will have more time for things such as love. Not forgetting about me of course." Seafra leaned heavily into Conall's legs.

"Things calming down - that has a nice ring to it. Yes, perhaps I will keep an extra watchful eye over her, but of course I'll try not to be obvious about it." Conall laid a shining, sharp arrow down on a nearby table. "There, that is the last arrow. This kingdom sure has an impressive amount of weapons. Should we see how the others fare? Maybe today will be the day we scout out the tunnels? Do you know if anyone found Jahari yet?"

"Sadly, no. With his ability to fly, there is no way to trace his tracks. We can only hope he returns, but I feel he is headed for Ethel. His broken heart could not bear another day without her I think. I can't imagine what it would feel like to not have you around. Whatever creates us ties us to our masters in a deep way. It would be like living with half a heart to have you taken away. Let us hope he will return safely."

"Yes, let us hope."

"Good morning, mighty man and mighty Seafra," Juliana said with a smile as she helped Derek put some rations into a brown sack.

"Good morning, Juliana." Conall did not yet refer to her as Mother. Maybe one day, she didn't seem to mind. "How are the preparations coming?"

"After I tie this bag, we are done."

"Done? That is what I like to hear on a warm, sunny morning," King Dem said, smiling lovingly at Juliana. "Akeyera and I are done also."

"Yes, we are," Akeyera said, joining the group, closely followed by Ida and Corbett. "I have organized the troops who will be coming with us, sixty in total. I thought we should bring more than a scouting party just in case Irenen is waiting for us, but according to my knowledge and Juliana's information, we will have nothing to worry about. We will send a scouting party ahead of the main group and split at the tunnel near the Dark Kingdom and send some to the Wooded Kingdom. The rest will stay here and continue restoring this kingdom."

Dem reached over patting Corbett on the back. Ida stood by Corbett's side. "We are sorry you will not be joining us, but we understand," Dem said.

"Yes, I would like to join you, but..." He gazed at Ida. "I could not part with Ida for that long again. I feel I could be of greater help here anyway with my woodworking abilities. I am not much of fighter. We will see all of you soon."

Ida walked over to Conall. "Return to me quickly, my son."

"I will, Mother. Don't you worry." He wrapped his wings around his mother as he hugged her.

The group of sixty gathered at the entrance of the barracks, their supplies in tow. "We will see you hopefully in a week's time or sooner," Conall said in a hopeful tone.

"Be safe, all of you," Ida said as they walked toward the tunnel entrance.

"Do you think they will rescue Ethel?" she whispered, laying her head on Corbett's shoulder, watching the others slowly disappear into the tunnel.

"I do, my love, I do."

Conall glanced back at Ida, remembering the last time he had done this same thing but with Ethel at his side. This time, however, Ida waved. He smiled. He knew he had to find Ethel. They stood where the strange creature had emerged only days ago. The area looked completely different. The pillars had been restored along with a large stone pathway leading to a service entrance into the tunnel system below.

"Tunnels," Conall said. "I don't see why anyone would ever want to build one, let alone a network of them. I wonder how long we will be down here before we reach the Dark Kingdom."

"I would say, judging by this map." Akeyera pointed to another stone map carved into the tunnel wall. "Probably at least five days, and that is if everything goes smoothly. The scouting party will go significantly quicker since the ten of you can fly. We will walk together for a day, which will be hard to distinguish down here, and then tomorrow the scouts can leave. Conall, you will lead the scouting team."

Conall stopped and stared in shock at Akeyera. "Me? Really? Wow, are you sure?"

"Yes, you are ready and have proven yourself. Just remember to pay attention and not to do anything reckless. You have others to think about." Akeyera looked intently into his eyes, causing him to fidget.

"It looks like we are all here. Follow me," Akeyera said.

With their lanterns lit, the sixty of them walked uneventfully until their eyelids began to droop and their legs grew weary.

"I think it is well into the evening. We will rest here for the night. There are small meals already prepared in the rations, or you can choose to sleep first and eat tomorrow morning. I am going to skip the meal and sleep," Akeyera said as she watched the others follow suit, lining the tunnel.

Two scouts set up on either end to take the first watch, their little lanterns providing a comfortable light in what would have been and impenetrable darkness. She could hear Seafra's deep breathing near her as she snuggled into her blanket, her eyes drifting over to Conall, who looked comfortably nestled into Seafra's fur. She wished she could join the two of them.

The first thing that greeted her was the smell of something delicious. She opened her eyes, forgetting where she was momentarily, then remembered they were in a tunnel.

"Good morning, Akeyera."

Akeyera stretched. "That smells delicious, Derek. Nobody ever woke me for my shift."

"No, the men took care of that for you. Conall's request." Derek winked at Akeyera, his finger to his lips. "Sit yourself down over here and help yourself to some fried eggs, strawberries, and rolls."

Akeyera smiled ever so slightly hearing Conall's request. Everyone around her seemed focused on either putting their gear away or eating, so she did not worry that anyone heard. "Derek, this is delicious. Thank you. I think Conall will do great leading the group. You will keep an eye on him, won't you?"

"Yes, don't worry. I will keep both eyes on him. He will do great. He is still young but has to start leading at some point, especially since he is the king's only son."

"True. Thank you. I think you should hurry back because your cooking talents will be greatly missed around here." Akeyera said with a smile.

"I have that all taken care of and have left instructions here with Tom, who will be more than capable of taking care of all of you. It will be his first time as lead in the kitchen. Wow, makes me feel old, but like I said, the young ones have to start leading at some point." Derek said.

"Yes, they do. I did. Here comes Conall. Looks like they are all ready, just missing one." She grabbed the dishes that Derek currently fussed over only to have them quickly snagged by Tom.

"Are you ready, Conall?" Akeyera asked.

"Yes. We needed our last person, and we seem to have found him." Conall elbowed Derek in the rib gently. "I will do my best to be back as quickly as possible. I have the copy of the map in my pocket, but I have it pretty much memorized. We will camp until you arrive, and hopefully by then we will have a good form of attack."

"Good luck, Conall. The men will listen, and, Conall..." She leaned into him and whispered, "Please be careful."

"I will," he whispered back, making sure no one was looking at the moment he reached around her slender frame and gave her a quick side hug, their secret love hidden from everyone except a select few.

King Demeerco smiled at a distance behind the two of them, proud of his son, hopeful that one day he would settle down with a queen, but now they must focus on rescuing Ethel. "You will do well, my son. See you soon."

"Thank you, Father. I will do my best."

Conall stood in front, the other nine men forming a line behind him. They opened their wings causing the dust to swirl around. It was an impressive sight to see the armor making strange pings of light bounce on the tunnel walls. Conall hovered for a moment, waiting for Titus to pick up Seafra, who had refused to stay behind with the others. They slipped quietly down the tunnel, the swoosh of their wings echoing until it could no longer be heard. Conall only paused twice to consult the map and then faster than he had expected, they arrived at what they were looking for—a small beam of light shining above and down into the tunnel where they all stood.

"Good time, Conall," Titus said. "I wasn't sure how much longer my arms would hold out."

"Are you calling me fat, Titus?" Seafra said with a friendly growl.

"No, just a little on the heavy side," Titus said with a wink.

Conall quietly surveyed the entrance above them. "It looks like we can fly up to get a good look at what is above us. I will go."

Conall reached the top quickly and grabbed the edge before stepping all the way out into the light. He was afraid Irenen would be waiting at the top with a sword. His heart pounded in his ears as he slowly poked his head out. A strange site greeted his eyes as they adjusted to the dim sunlight. Irenen's dark castle stood off in the distance. The destruction of the land was seen everywhere, but this area seemed untouched. A little pocket of what this ancient realm had once been like, somehow intact in this dark kingdom. A weeping willow swayed its happy green leaves in the light breeze. He lingered for a moment to make sure it was safe and pulled himself out of the well. As he cautiously moved around the area, he saw no signs of life outside of this little pocket anywhere. He wondered if anyone could see him from the dark, lifeless windows of the castle. As he made another slow round around the willow, he noticed footprints. He got on all fours and looked closer. He knew these prints. "Ethel," he whispered, and the willow shook ever so slightly. He rushed back to the well.

"What did you find up there? Did you see anyone?" Seafra growled.

"It actually looks pretty deserted. I think we may have some luck, or something is on our side, because I think the footprints I see around here are Ethel's. If she is coming around this area, we will be able to hear her. We will camp just beyond the well's entrance and send one of us up every so often."

The others set up a makeshift camp and waited, whispering quietly to each other of days gone by to pass the time as they waited for the others to come.

The red, pink, and orange beams struck each of the weeping willow's leaves in such a way that it seemed golden sparkles danced on the rims. Ethel stared at the vibrant living thing before her, ax pointed toward the dirt. The leaves seemed alive as they flitted in the light breeze in this distant kingdom corner. She gazed and began playing a game where the color had to move to the next leaf before the last beam disappeared. She paused, her mind flooded with memories. Her memories! She had played this game with that boy—Conall—her...twin brother!

Oh, what a happy moment, but a strange thing occurred in her as she realized the trickery Irenen had used on her to make her believe he was her father. She did not get angry. A smirk stayed on her pouty red lips as she left the tree, a word placing and nestling itself in her mind: power. What slipped by her as she focused on that word—power—was a large crumbling well now relegated to just another hole gaping up from the ground in the Dark Kingdom, which is probably why she didn't think twice about the hole. But this hole was different. A head poked through, covered in dust. A sun's ray strained to shine its light on the subject. A glint of golden hair sparked in the last beam and waved in the light breeze. Conall froze, his heart pounding as he watched the back of Ethel pause, and then she continued on her way. He laid his beloved hunting knife down near the base of the surprisingly living willow tree, hoping it would spark a memory in his sister. He gazed at her, wishing he could call out and all would go back to how it had been, but that would never be; too many things had passed. He reluctantly lowered himself down the well.

"Let us hope this works. This is the second time she has visited this area. We can only hope she will return and remember something."

"It will, Conall. Somehow it will," Seafra said quietly to himself.

Loud whispering ebbed down the tunnel, and they froze. Titus ran to the end of the tunnel, carrying a dimly lit lantern. As they held their breath, Titus said, "It's the others—they are coming."

Conall and the others let out a sigh of relief. It had been at least six days since they had left the others, and he was beginning to worry. He walked into the main tunnel, and the others greeted him.

"Akeyera," Conall said, "we were beginning to worry. Did something happen? Wait, you're bleeding."

"Don't worry. It is nothing. We encountered a smaller one of of those clear-skinned creatures only to have the tunnel crash behind us. The creature is dead, we made sure of that, but I am afraid we will have to find another way back. What have you found down here? Anything useful?"

"I am glad you are all right. I am sure this map will show us other access points we could use to get home. We have had a stroke of luck. Ethel visited the area above only a few moments ago. I have laid something up on the surface that will hopefully spark her memories. I just hope it is enough to do the trick."

"Don't worry, Conall. This plan will work. I can feel it." Akeyera rested a hand on Conall's shoulder, warmth spreading through her as Conall's large hand rested atop hers.

17

HOME

Morning dawned for the second morning since Akeyera and the others had arrived, sooner than Akeyera felt it should come. But she welcomed the sunlight that slid its way down the well into the tunnel. Everyone sat quietly eating a light breakfast, for fear anything cooked would be smelled above.

"When was the last day Ethel visited this area?" Akeyera inquired between mouthfuls of bread.

"Two days ago. I hoped she would come the next day—"

Everyone froze as the signal at the other end of the tunnel flashed, which meant someone was above.

Ethel had come to the willow once again with her ax. This time she meant business. It had become obvious to her that Irenen was not coming back, so she had changed a few things in the kingdom already, which surprisingly had made her subjects more loyal to her. The first thing she did was release the prisoners. She wanted to show people she cared. Then she focused on making more adequate living areas for all the servants. She assigned new roles and made new leaders, among other things. It had taken two very long days to get everybody organized and doing the different tasks. This kingdom was hers, and unlike Irenen, people would like her first, then fear her.

Now to take care of this annoying living thing. She raised her ax. The tree seemed to shiver, and before she could swing, the sun glinted off something on the ground that momentarily blinded her. She dropped the ax heavily and jumped toward the annoying blinding light near an insignificant hole. She recognized this small dagger. "Conall?" she whispered. A tear slid down her cheek.

Conall saw his opportunity. He pounced on his sister, surrounding her in a cloth bag and pulled her through the old well.

"Hey, let me go! Unhand me! Demerell, if that is you, I am going to destroy you and my father, who, by the way, is not my father. Let me go!"

Conall struggled to contain the small yet exceedingly powerful Ethel.

"Shh...Ethel, it is me, your brother, Conall."

"Careful, Conall," Seafra snarled loudly at Ethel as she kicked her feet.

He lifted the bag off her head as Titus, Akeyera, and Demeerco kept a tight grip on her.

Recognition flashed through Ethel at the sight of Conall.

"Conall, it is you?" She reached out a cautious hand to touch his face. "I thought it was just another trick of Irenen's."

The others continued to hold Ethel but a little more loosely.

"You recognize me?"

"Yes. I started to remember bits and pieces of what Irenen had tried to erase, and then your dagger, and, well, they all came flooding back. I apologize for what happened, but I was not myself."

"You are forgiven," Conall said, quickly hugging his sister.

"It is good to see you," Seafra said gruffly.

"Yes, so good to see you," the others chimed in.

"Father?"

"Yes, Ethel. Here, let us have a look at you."

Akeyera and Dem carefully looked Ethel over. She had a few bruises that were healing, but other than that she seemed herself.

"You look like you have fared well these past few months. How do you feel? Do you feel ready to start our journey home?"

"Home. That has nice ring to it. Yes, I feel mostly myself. A little in shock at seeing all of you. I honestly didn't think this day would happen."

"We are going to keep a close eye on you. Your hands will be tied, and Titus and Timothy will be assigned to be near you at all times. We must take precautions even if you do feel fine. You do understand, right?"

Ethel stopped herself. She could feel anger rising within her, wanting to lash out at the thought of being contained. How dare they treat a queen in such a way. But she could not let that side of her out, not at a time like this. She did need a few things before she departed. "Oh, yes, I understand, but I can't leave Jahari behind."

"Jahari? He made it?"

"Yes. Although he does not seem quite how I remember him, but I could go back and get him. It won't raise any suspicion since I fly often. I would need to go alone though." She gauged their reactions, hoping she could go alone, not wanting to tell them of Irenen's disappearance for fear they would be more likely come with her.

"I don't know—"

"You can trust me. I am better, see." She held out her arms toward her father for a hug. He carefully allowed her to hug him, a little unsure of what to expect, and to his surprise, nothing happened.

"I must say that finding you was a lot easier than any of us expected. If we do allow you to go, where will you meet us? Our path is blocked the way we came. We will have to find a new route back, and it would be quicker above ground if we all fly."

"I have explored the kingdom pretty thoroughly, and there is a small worn road just east of that willow tree up there. You can see it if you stand behind the large boulder next to that annoying will...I mean pile of rocks. See, it is very much hidden." Ethel held in a snarl over the slipup and not being rid of the living willow tree. "I will get Jahari and be back by tonight's moon."

"It feels strange to let you leave, having just found you, but I trust you. Jahari is needed. Poor fellow probably needs us. You will need your hands to fly, so we will not tie you when you get back, but Titus and Timothy will be assigned to watch you. Hurry back quickly, my daughter." Dem hugged Ethel tightly.

Then she was gone up the well. As she walked briskly, she smiled. This life without Irenen was working out better than she expected. She would grab a few of her beloved items, find the emotionally distant Jahari, and return before nightfall.

"Do you think she is really all right?" Conall asked.

"I think she will need healing just as Juliana has but not as intense. She has only been gone for six months or so. Has it really already been six months?" Dem said while shaking his head in disbelief. "Time does move faster than we would like. We arrived here as quickly as we could. I think she will make a fast recovery. I would like to send a scouting group to the Wooded Kingdom still. I will send the others through the tunnel that Ethel did not see. I want to keep our military strategies secret from her for the time being."

"That is wise," Derek said.

"Looks like you have a good crew in this tunnel, awaiting orders." Derek patted Akeyera on the shoulder.

The five men stood in impressive armor, ready for their orders. "We are ready, Akeyera, and have consulted the map several times. We will arrive at the Wooded Kingdom in two days' time," one of the scouting party said.

"I look forward to your return, hopefully with good information on how the Wooded Kingdom has fared."

"We will return quickly." The five men began their walk in the direction of the Wooded Kingdom until Akeyera could no longer see their lantern bobbing along the tunnel.

"The rest of you follow me," she said. "We will wait above ground in the shrubs for Ethel."

The fifty-five soldiers exited the tunnel cautiously, hiding themselves near the old path in the shrubs. Seafra struggled to get out with the strange angle, but eventually he and Titus spilled out of the tunnel into the last rays of dim sunlight. They quickly hid themselves with the others, hearts pounding for fear they had been spotted. They breathed a sigh of relief when the only sound was the breeze in the willow. Dark began to fall.

"I am worried about Ethel," Conall said. "Maybe one of us should go find her."

"Patience, Conall. It is barely nightfall. She will be here." Dem said this more to himself than to Conall.

They heard a crunch directly in front of them. The clouds had moved in and provided the extra cover they needed. Ethel had returned with Jahari. Seafra instantly recognized Jahari. He stepped out from cover and stared at Jahari. Jahari lifted his head in recognition, his eyes sparkling, and he trotted a little faster to their location. No one dared to speak for fear of being discovered, and when they were a safe distance away, all fifty-five lifted into the air and flew toward the Forgotten Kingdom. The few sparks of starlight glinted off the different pieces of armory. Conall kept a watchful eye on Ethel while trying to keep his focus on not dropping Seafra.

"Conall, I am slipping," Seafra said.

"No, you are not. You just think you are. We are almost there anyway. Why do you have to be such a large wolf?"

"I am large because that is who I am. I want my own set of wings so I don't ever have to do this again."

"Ha, that would be nice for the both of us." Conall smiled down at Seafra, and he smiled back, their bond inseparable.

"Thank you, Conall," Seafra whispered into the night air.

"You are welcome. I wouldn't want to do this without you. I don't mind carrying you if that means you can be a part of us. Does Jahari seem strange to you?" Conall whispered the last part so quietly that Seafra barely heard him.

"I did catch a glimpse of his eyes, and the old Jahari is inside. I can see him shining through. I think maybe he is keeping something from us. Not sure. At the right time, I am sure he will reveal to us what he is really thinking."

They flew until the sun began to rise. They had made incredible time with the wind helping them along the way. A bright light jumped in the first beam of sunlight far ahead.

Akeyera turned over so she flew with her back toward the ground, facing the others. "Can all of you hang in there another hour or two? That glinting ahead, that is the castle. We are almost there. If you need to rest, just let me know."

Nobody said they wanted to land, and not flying again for a long while sounded amazing to them. The sight of the castle energized everyone, and they flew harder, arriving on the doorsteps of castle just before noon. They all landed heavily, happy to stretch their legs and rest their tired wings.

"Ethel, welcome to the Forgotten Kingdom. I am the princess of this beautiful place."

Ethel stood at the footsteps of the large castle that glowed a deep gold in the sun. "I wondered at the direction we had been going. When I heard home, I assumed the Wooded Kingdom was where we were headed."

"Ah, yes, I should have clarified our new home. We are unsure of the condition of the Wooded Kingdom at this time." Dem said this with a cautious eye on Ethel. He couldn't pinpoint his unease around her, but something made him uncomfortable.

Ida stepped out of the door.

"Mother?" Ethel involuntarily lurched forward.

Titus and Timothy put their hands in front of her to stop her. Her sudden urge to hug Ida surprised herself.

"Oh, you found Ethel." Ida approached more slowly than she wished, wanting nothing more than to run with open arms to hug her beautiful daughter.

Titus and Timothy allowed the two to embrace. Ida grabbed her and hugged tightly. The entire party made their way into the castle. The soldiers were quickly ushered away by different servants to be put to bed.

Everyone went happily to their different rooms. Only Ethel, Conall, Dem, Ida, and Akeyera stayed behind to be shortly joined by Corbett and Juliana. They stood chatting happily, as if time had been frozen and all that they had experienced was but a dream.

"Excuse me, all you lovely people." Queen Anna stood dressed in a regal blue gown flowing over her ample yet shapely body. "We would like to throw a party welcoming everyone back. But only if you think all of you will be up to it."

Everyone in the room stared at Akeyera. "I think I feel up to it, but what do you think, Ethel?"

"I think that sounds like a grand idea."

"Then let us get all of you to bed and rested for tomorrow."

18

LIFE ETERNAL

The morning dawned bright and warm. Ethel stretched and yawned, lazily rolling to her side to stare out an open window. Her lavish room was on the first floor. She walked over to the window and took a deep breath of fresh air. For a moment, her old self seethed forward, shaking the prison of herself within. Feeling as if she was a kingdom forgotten, she stared into Jahari's face for a moment, grabbing his cheeks. A silent escape of air filled the space between them. "Find me, Jahari."

"I will, my princess. I will." He nudged her hand gently.

There was a gentle knock on her door, and as quickly as she had surfaced, she was gone. "Come in. I am awake." She wiped away her tears, which had become a common morning occurrence for her.

"Good morning, Ethel! Time to get up. We have a big day today. Come, sleepyhead," Ida said in a nice but demanding tone, her green eyes glinting in the sun. "Oh, and Jahari, too. I should've guessed you would be at her window. Always keeping a watchful eye on her. What a good companion you have, Ethel."

Ethel looked at Jahari, but her eyes were empty. "I know he is."

"The palace has been a busy place while you have been sleeping the morning away, and we have much to do. I am here to get you ready. And, Jahari, you have been requested in the stables—you have attire to wear. So off you go."

Ethel felt unease growing in her as Jahari hesitated to leave her side, or did he seem eager to leave her side? She couldn't tell for sure. She licked her lips, feeling exceedingly thirsty all of the sudden. "Umm...yes. Go, Jahari. And, Mother, excuse me a moment while I freshen up."

"Oh, why, yes, of course. I will get your jewelry ready, and a few ladies will join us to help you with your gorgeous green gown and a few of the other things that go with getting ready. I must get ready also. Now, shoo, freshen up so we may start."

Ethel gave a sideways look at Jahari, who moved too quickly from the window for her liking, but at the moment, her mind screamed for her purple elixir. She shut the bathroom door behind her, happy that she had time to hide a few of her important items throughout her room before falling asleep last night. Standing on her tiptoes, she reached the top of a cupboard, and a cool glass jar greeted her fingertips. She uncapped the bottle, its intoxicating fumes filling her nostrils. She looked deep into her blue glass bottle. The desire to drink it all overwhelmed her. "Pace yourself, Ethel," she said. She took a few sips and returned the bottle. This would last her a little while, but she would need more soon. She looked at herself in the mirror and smiled.

"I am ready. Sorry it took me so long."

"It didn't take you long at all." Ladies began fussing over Ethel and Ida, chatting all the while of the exciting festivities to come.

Jahari walked quickly to the stables. On seeing his friends awaiting him, he ran to them, knowing Ethel would not see him. "Oh, Seafra, Conall, Dem, how I have missed you." He pushed his head lovingly on all of them.

"Jahari, there you are. You have been so quiet," Conall said.

"I know. I..." Jahari looked around and began to whisper. "Ethel is not herself. She is trapped inside herself, screaming inside to be let out, but I have yet to find a way to help her. Before Irenen left, she began to—"

"Wait, what? Irenen left? Ethel didn't mention that," Dem said, shock on his face.

"No, she wouldn't. This new Ethel is power hungry with Irenen gone. I have seen it grow in her. He and Demerell left a few days ago, and nobody has heard from them. I have been doing my best to keep close to her, but it is hard. She is suspicious. I do know that Irenen had her drinking a purple liquid, and she may have brought some with her. It keeps her in kind of a controlled state of madness if that makes sense."

"Oh, Jahari, thank you for this information. We thought you were gone to us. Hmm...I wonder if our scouting party has encountered Irenen on the way to the Wooded Kingdom. It is still too soon for them to have returned," Dem said.

"They may have met him, but he would not pose much of a threat. He was sickly when he left. But Demerell would have. There was a rumor in the Dark Kingdom that Irenen sought a golden bush that would give him unending life," Jahari said with a snort.

Conall's face grew white with a forgotten memory. He reached out and steadied himself on Dem's shoulder.

"Conall? What is it?" Dem asked, concern etching his voice.

"I know that bush."

Everyone stared quietly in anticipation, waiting for Conall to speak.

"That first day I saw you, Dem, and you cut those ropes from Akeyera, I remember seeing a sprout of golden leaves weaving itself from the ropes you cut. Irenen is going to where we first met. I don't know how he knows of that place, but we have to stop him."

"We will. After tonight's party, we will sneak away, only telling a few of what we are doing and hopefully we find the scouting party on the way," Dem said, his mind already formulating a plan.

"We can make good time flying. Seafra, do you still want to come?" Conall asked.

"Of course! Especially if it aids us in our quest, Ethel might be suspicious if she sees me here without you since we are hardly ever separate," Seafra growled.

"With that settled, Jahari, can you maintain your course of action with Ethel?" Dem said in a serious tone.

"Yes, I will do my best as she continues to grow more suspicious. This will be the last time I will talk with you about such things unless there is another party where she's occupied the entire day."

"We have much to do before the party." Dem instructed them on whom to tell, setting up a solid plan before they went their separate ways until the party that evening.

"Jahari, you look amazing," Ethel said as she greeted him through the open window. Her elegant curls danced in the afternoon breeze.

Jahari stood regally, staring into Ethel's eyes, once again a hint of joy hidden in their depths. His golden armor clinked as he shifted his wings. "I am not used to wearing anything. But this is surprisingly lightweight. My personal favorite is the way the diamonds sparkle on my wings. They did an amazing job when they designed this fanciful armor. And you, Ethel, you are breathtaking."

She smiled as she spun in her sparkling green gown. Shimmering sapphires and rubies danced in her hair and off her elegant neckline. "I thought the Wooded Kingdom had wealth. This is like nothing I have ever seen before. I could get comfortable here." Her joyous smiled wavered ever so slightly.

"Oh, Ethel, you look amazing!" Ida said.

"Wow, you do, too. The color of your gown is nothing I have ever seen before, almost as if they captured the rays of a golden sunset. Looks beautiful with your red hair."

"I know. It is beautiful. Are you ready to join the party?"

The other ladies stood beaming at the two of them, proud of their walking masterpieces.

"I am, but what would you think of riding in on Jahari and making a grand entrance?"

The other ladies in the room balked at the idea.

"Good ladies," one said, "it is not becoming to climb out the window."

But her words had no power, and the two of them sat smiling on top of an already trotting Jahari. Their dresses glinted in sunbeams, combining with Jahari's diamonds, sent a cascade of dancing color around them. Titus and Timothy quickly entered the room and jumped out the window to follow, not far behind.

"I didn't see that coming," Titus said, trying to catch his breath.

"Neither did I. Let us hope that is all the surprises we have for the night."

Jahari slowed to a graceful walk with his head held high, proud to carry such beautiful ladies. He hoped that somehow tonight would free Ethel's mind. He pranced around the corner.

"Ida, you look positively amazing." Corbett helped her down, his face beaming as she grabbed his arm.

"Of course I do," Ida said with a playful grin. "You do as well, my dear." They kissed and joined the party.

The lavishness of the party surrounded everything, from the plush chairs to the glittering decorations. Every guest was adorned in the finest clothes. Seafra and Jahari stood out from the crowd, and everyone wanted to talk to talking beasts. Their finery made them look elegant yet fierce. The party went into the wee hours of the night until the moonlight danced off the plentiful fountains.

"Come, come. We must all sing the closing song to commemorate such a spectacular party and wonderful new and old friends." King Tarius said this loudly, standing on a stone bench to get the large group's attention.

"Ethel, dear, come stand by me. You look troubled. Is something wrong?" Ida said, hoping her eyes didn't give away what she already knew.

"I was going to stand next to Conall and Dem but can't seem to find them or Seafra." Ethel stood on her tiptoes, searching the night-covered crowd. Torches were lit and stars shining, but the dim light proved useless in her search.

"Don't worry. I am sure they are around."

"Yes, I am sure," she said with the slightest hiss in her voice. Ida shivered.

Dem, Conall, Seafra, and Derek quietly slipped away into the night air as the start of the song drifted to their ears.

"There is a part of me that wishes we could've stayed and left tomorrow," Conall said.

"Me too, Conall. It will be a party to remember. We will be back before you know it, and I am sure there will be another party. From what I remember about this kingdom, they love a good party." Dem's white teeth glinted in the moonlight. They began their quiet journey to the golden bush with hopes of finding what they searched for.

"What a glorious evening, one to be remembered for sure. I do believe I will retire and sleep until tomorrow night." She spun around in her gown, watching it shimmer. "I am glad we are together again," Ida said happily.

"Yes, I will remember this night for a long time. I am happy to be with you again also." Ethel said.

"Good night. Sleep comfortably." Ida gave Ethel a big hug and lingered a moment happy to be alive and with her daughter.

"I will sleep comfortably, you as well." Ethel was escorted to her room by Timothy and Titus.

"May I speak to Conall?" she said this a little more demanding than she had wanted.

"My good lady, he has retired for the night, and Dem has joined Juliana for the night. Perhaps it would please you to see them in the morning?"

"It will please me not!" They stared unmoving at her, their hands on the pommels of their swords. "Forgive me. I am tired. I will retire for the night."

Ethel closed the door behind her. She walked over to shut her window. "Good night, Jahari," she said coldly, a burning thirst suddenly gripping her where she stood as she touched the window frame.

"Are you all right, Ethel?" Concern etched Jahari's features, and it made Ethel mad.

"I am fine. Good night, Jahari!" She shut the window, trying not to slam it, and quickly walked to her hidden bottle. She paused and turned around; she felt like somebody was watching her. Nobody was around, so she took a long sip. Jahari watched through a crack in the window, then, when Ethel looked away, he knelt down and kept watch under her window.

Ethel wiped her mouth on her sleeve and quietly stepped into her room, which was shared by an open door with Akeyera. Guards stood outside both of their doors. The room was empty except for the guards outside her door.

Ethel stepped onto the ornate marble-carved balcony through Akeyera's room, staring at the beautiful, unfamiliar land, not noticing Jahari, who had concealed himself along the wall. She took a deep breath of night air, allowing the cold liquid to trickle down her insides. A small smirk crossed her lips. "This is working out better than I could have ever hoped," she whispered.

Before crawling into her plush bed, she reached between the mattress and frame, looking for what she had quickly hidden before anyone could see. Her hand rested for a moment on a cold steel blade, making its way to rest on the majestic ruby hilt. A thought began to weave itself through her mind. Looking around, all was silent around her room. She gently pushed the window open, and the chatter of voices could be heard on the night air from the party. She dropped to the cold hard ground with a soft plop and suddenly froze. "Oh, Jahari, you startled me. I just needed a little breath of fresh air."

"Ethel, I am no dumb beast. You are preparing to leave. Get back in your room before I shout for help." As he spoke the last of these words, a blur of motion came from Ethel, and her cold steel blade cut through his beautiful hide, enough to draw blood on his leg.

"Jahari, I'm sorr...No, never mind, I'm not. You have been sneaking around here and you will take me to where the others have gone, or so help me, I will punish you for what you have done," she whispered sharply, tears spilling down her cheeks.

"If I refuse, will you kill your friend? Ethel, remember who you are, please remember." Jahari choked the words out as Ethel began to push the blade on his throat.

"Death, no. How does chained around your wings in a cage sound? While being surrounded by flying creatures day and night? The Ethel you speak of is gone, you have me or nothing."

Jahari felt ashamed for what he was about to do, but the thought of a lifetime of captivity with no hope of ever freeing Ethel from her internal prison made him reluctantly agree to help her. He knew his help would aid her in escaping unseen. His sword wound on his leg made his flesh throb. He limped behind Ethel as they quietly made their way to a secluded spot where they could fly away unseen.

"Ethel, before you get on, is there anything you could do for my leg?" He was unsure of how she would respond.

"Oh, of course." Quickly, before he could jump away, she poured a few drops of purple liquid on his wound. He felt his mind becoming cloudy, but his leg stopped throbbing. His shame for not being able to say no to Ethel still radiated in his chest. He tried to speak but his cloudy mind prevented it. They flew for a few days, the scent of the others guiding Jahari. Even when he tried to resist Ethel's direction, he couldn't. It was as if she controlled him somehow with that purple liquid on his leg.

"Jahari, I recognize this area as if it were from a distant dream. This is the spot Conall and I first entered the Wooded Kingdom. Let us land there in that clearing for the night. Tomorrow is the day we will find that bush."

Jahari with reluctant obedience landed, and they rested for the night. As the cool summer dawned, a warped kind of giddy joy coursed through Ethel's purple veins as she drank the last drop of her purple liquid. Her eyes rested on Jahari, who stood facing her, ready, his leg a strange purple color. A quick pang of sadness pricked her heart. She pushed the feeling aside.

"Come, Jahari, today is going to be a grand day. No longer will I rely on that purple drink; today is the day I will forever live."

"Ethel, careful," Jahari mumbled quietly, still not able to find his voice.

Throwing caution aside, Ethel raced toward the bush, knowing it was up ahead. She burst through the trees and abruptly stopped. There standing before her were two familiar-looking statues.

"Ha, I recognize you statues. Looks like it didn't go as you expected, Irenen and Demerell. It will go better for me though." She laughed a crazy laugh, which died on her tongue as Irenen's eyes outlined in stone moved in her direction. A shiver shook her body. She held her sword pointed at the living statue.

"Ethel, don't do this!" Conall shouted from the edge of the trees.

In her excitement, she had failed to notice not only the party who flew out but also the scouting party, who all stood in a semicircle not that far from her. She spun around, her silver sword glinting in the sun.

"Conall? Why don't you come over here and stop me! Or are all of you some strange figment of my imagination?"

"I assure you they are not. I am sorry, Conall, but I could not resist her," Jahari said, finding his voice. Conall lightly patted his side in understanding.

"We will not interfere, Ethel. But look at what that bush did to the two others. Is that the kind of eternal life you desire? Please don't do this," Conall begged as they all began to inch forward.

"Jahari, you traitor!" Before anyone could react, she moved with inhumanly speed and yanked a golden leaf.

She blinked hard as a flash of golden light pulsated around her, causing everything to fade, an image wriggled faintly near her as a memory came to life of the moment when the bush first appeared. She stood next to her former self. Her old self turned to her, its hand reaching out, the unseeing eyes glowing white. Her hand reached in response and paused. The image grew stronger but then it began to waver, a voice radiated from the ghostlike Ethel. "Choose right," it whispered.

Her hand went down and gripped the ruby hilt by her hip. The power she desired seemed to be fading. She shook her head, tightening her grip. "No!" She lashed out at the image. The dreamlike image disappeared, and she once again stood by the bush, holding the powerful golden leaf. She beamed at the faces around her, her smile wavering as the faces around her stared back in shock.

"Why do you look at me so? Am I not the one that will rule you? See, I am different than these other two. The bush has decided that my everlasting life will not take statue form." She raised her breathtaking blade to the sky, face upturned in complete dark joy. "I will and forever will be Queen Ethel, ruler of all. This leaf will adorn my crown." She looked down at her hand and stopped. She cried out in horror as she realized what was happening. Her slender hand was becoming misshapen and twisting in the shape of a white tree branch. Panicked, she shouted, "I'm sorry, I will choose whatever you offered before! Come back, wake me from this living nightmare. Please don't do this!"

A quiet, wind like voice emanated from the bush. "You decided."

She watched tears spilling from her eyes as her body somehow transformed itself into the shape of the tree she had wanted to cut down, the weeping willow. The sword became a shining branch reaching toward the sky, her branchlike hand permanently entwined around it. She fought the transformation but gave in as she realized nothing could be done. She had chosen wrong. The faces around her drew close. She could feel pressure on her body as they tried to free her to no avail.

Conall's face was in front of hers. "If we can, we will find a way to reverse this." He hugged her now-smooth bark.

Her mind felt sluggish, full of thoughts of life, green things that wanted living water. More tears slid down her bark-enclosed face, becoming sap as they trickled down. "No, Conall, this is best for all of us. Irenen did something to me that I don't think can ever be reversed. My everlasting life will be spent drinking the living water that runs beneath my deep roots. Tell Mother, Jahari...everyone that I am sorry. I love you so..." At that moment, the white bark of the tree claimed Ethel as a part of itself.

Conall dropped to his knees in disbelief. Thoughts began racing through his mind - how could his sister have chosen so wrongly? Perhaps if he could've come sooner maybe this would not have happened? He pounded his fists into the ground and let out an anguished cry. Tears streamed freely down his cheeks. "Why, Ethel why did you choose this and leave me? We could've helped you." He whispered quietly.

He slowly stood and shot an angry glance at Irenen's statue. "All of this is your fault!" He stood in front of the statue and kicked at the cold stone. "I see your cold calculating eyes moving and I'm not sure how you are still alive under that stone, but it seems a fitting punishment for all the things you have done." Conall walked over to

Ethel and hugged her not wanting to ever let go. He was joined by the others and they all hugged Ethel.

"Conall, it is time to leave. We will come back and build a wall to protect this area later. You must let go. Maybe one day we will discover a way to reverse this, but we have much to do. Both kingdoms need us, and the Dark Kingdom will need a new ruler if they are willing." He patted Conall on the shoulder, pulling him gently. "Come, son, what would I tell Ida if you did not return with us? Telling her and the others of this will be hard enough. We have much to do, and there are kingdoms that need their kings."

Conall's puffy red eyes stared one last time at his almost unrecognizable sister, knowing Dem was right: he could not stay here. "One day, Ethel, we will reverse this. I love you," he whispered as he hugged her trunk, his wings wrapping around it. He hoped that would heal her, but it did nothing.

They stood staring at Ethel, and one by one, they started their trek back to the Forgotten Kingdom, hearts torn between the joys of the Wooded Kingdom not being destroyed and losing a loved one to something they didn't understand. They slowly walked away until all that was left was the sound of rustling leaves and a pair of eyes, outlined in stone, staring back at the living weeping willow. Dark eyes that blinked with quiet cunningness.

Made in the USA
Charleston, SC
23 October 2014